# LIONESS OF
# PUNJAB

# LIONESS OF
# PUNJAB

ANITA JARI KHARBANDA

YALI BOOKS
NEW YORK

Published by Yali Books, New York

Text © 2022 by Anita Jari Kharbanda
Cover Art by Anantjeet Kaur

Connect with us online:
**yalibooks.com**
Social: @yalibooks

Library of Congress Control Number: 2022934882

ISBN: 978-1-949528-71-8

978-1-949528-69-5 (eBook)

Typeset in Maiola and Calder

*To my mother, Aruna Sikand Jari, and my father, Atamjit Singh Jari—You guided me with steady hands and loving hearts. You were warriors, exemplifying sacrifice, hard work, and duty.*

*And to my husband, Viney, and my sons, Yuvraj and Shaan—May you remain warriors of the heart and mind.*

# PROLOGUE

Mai Bhago. Bhag Bhari. Bhag Kaur. I have been blessed with many names. They say when I was born, a mighty scream was heard across our village of Jhabal Kalan in Punjab. Some even claim that the cry traveled to the holy city of Amritsar and caused quite a stir. It was a sound unlike anything the villagers had heard before—a guttural scream that promised to avenge their suffering. My pitaji knew that a feared daughter of God, a dhi of Waheguru, was born that day, and he named me Bhag Bhari, fortune-filled. Anointed a Sikh as a kuri, I took on the name of Bhag Kaur, Princess of Fortune. Much later in life, I was revered as the formidable Mata Bhag Kaur. But you, you may call me—and remember me as—Mai Bhago.

I grew up in the seventeenth century in war-torn Hindustan, when my people in Punjab were battling the might of the Mughal Army, commanded by Emperor Aurangzeb. The Mughal dynasty had reigned over Hindustan for more than a century, bringing people of many religions under Islamic rule. But under Aurangzeb, this patchwork empire was at war with itself. My people, followers of the peace-loving Guru Nanak, were a small community united by our beliefs. Guru Nanak never intended to create a new religion. He named us his *sikhs*, or students. He sought peace, carving out a spiritual path that veered away from the two dominant religions of Hinduism and Islam. Yet, by the time I was born, Sikhs were seen as a threat to the emperor's throne in Delhi, and we were tormented at every turn.

Tired of being punished for our beliefs, we fought back. Our men rode into battle, leaving their families behind to fend for themselves. Often, the men never returned, and women kept their children fed and clothed, raising their sons to become future warriors. This was how many Sikh families lived, and I was raised to be a devout Sikh woman.

But it was a simple fact: I was not a kuri of my time. From when I could remember, the thought of my people being killed angered me. I would not accept my fate as a woman, left behind in the villages to mourn. I was going to fight. This was a promise I made to myself.

# ONE

It was a bright day in the thirteenth summer after I was born, and as the sun spread its benevolent warmth over our Punjabi village, Mataji and Pitaji left for the bazaar in a nearby town to barter for wares. Their absence allowed us siblings time to explore uncharted territory.

My veere, my brothers, pushed aside the reed screen hiding the treasures of our brick home—our pitaji's weapons. We quickly tossed aside the jute mats on top, revealing sharp-edged bracelets, deadly little daggers, bows, and shiny arrows. We dug until the weapon we sought revealed itself to us. I gingerly unraveled a sheathed blade from the blankets it lay wrapped in, sending a thrill down my spine. I ignored my brothers' requests to touch the sword. Dilbagh was born the summer after me, and Bhag, or Chotu, two winters after me. And as their bhenji, elder sister, I had to protect them. But more than that, I wanted to keep the weapon to myself. Gripping the sword by its hilt, I carefully unsheathed the kirpan and held it up in front of us. My hand trembled beneath the weight of the blade. It had a sharp, unfamiliar odor—perhaps old blood?

"I didn't expect it to be so heavy. Pitaji must be stronger than he looks." I glanced at Chotu, who stared wide-eyed at the blade glinting in the sunlight streaming in from the small window above us.

"It reeks of death. Look at the crusty dark parts. That is dried blood . . . and maybe flesh. How many warriors do you think Pitaji slew with this mighty sword?" Dilbagh's eyes locked on the kirpan, and his eyebrows came together in concentration.

"Ja!" Chotu snapped as he waved a pretend sword in the air. "He must have slain many!" His amiable face glowed with pride.

"Chotu, Pitaji fought tyranny alongside our Guru. Killing is not something to take lightly," I chided him, sliding the blade back into its protective sheath.

"Yes, we know. You sound just like Mataji, dear Bhen." Dilbagh continued in a squeaky voice, "War is a last resort, and we fight with honor." He picked up a bow and fingered the leather grip, running his thumb over the smooth bands, before he spoke again in his normal low tone, "The war is never going to end, and Pitaji is too old to fight." He tossed the bow back onto the pile. "And Chotu and I are too young."

I felt a twinge of irritation. "Don't tease me, gadha. I am your elder sister." But his teasing wasn't why I called him a donkey.

"Maybe you should fight, Bhenji? You're more of a man than half the boys in the village," said Dilbagh in a sly voice.

He laughed at his own joke. I ground my teeth. "Only more of a man than a little weakling like you." I shoved Dilbagh with more force than necessary. He jerked back and rubbed his chest, glaring at me. Dilbagh raised his arm to slap me, but Chotu intercepted, gripping his arm in mid-air.

"Go outside, so you don't break anything."

We rewrapped Pitaji's weapons and rushed out into the yard. In his hurry, Chotu bumped into the chulha. Ashes shot up from the horseshoe-shaped clay stove in a puff and covered our bare feet.

"Oy, watch where you're going!" I coughed and dusted off my feet. "Look at this mess."

Dilbagh sprinted ahead and jumped onto our tree swing. I charged at him, and he met me head-on. We grunted as we clenched handfuls of each other's clothing and wrestled each other to the ground. My veer fell beneath me, and I released my right hand to jab him in the ribs. He let go and grabbed my hair with both hands. As I tried to yank his hands off my hair, Dilbagh wriggled out from beneath me, and Chotu pounced on top of him. I inserted myself back into the fray and jabbed my elbow into Chotu's back, pushing him off our brother. I wanted to be the one to take Dilbagh down.

"Oyyyy!" Chotu writhed in pain. "I thought we had a bhen, not a veer." He rolled off and rubbed his back.

If they thought calling me a man would make me stop fighting, they were about to find out otherwise.

Dilbagh jumped to his feet and headbutted me in the stomach. I almost tripped over a bulging tree root, but I shuffled my feet to regain my balance.

"Pagal!" I clutched my stomach and doubled over. As Dilbagh neared, I quickly stuck my leg out to knock him off his feet. He fell to the ground with a thump. Puffs of dirt flew into the air, and he shifted uncomfortably on the uneven ground beneath him. But he didn't give up. Grabbing a few stones from a pile of rocks, he threw them at me, but he missed by several feet.

"You won't be able to shoot arrows with that aim," I snickered, and rubbed my sore stomach.

The three of us were lying on the ground licking our wounds, covered in dirt and sweat, when Mataji and Pitaji returned. Mataji was carrying bales of fabric, while Pitaji held up two clay pots. I held my breath as Mataji approached us, her earth-colored salwar-kameez and gauzy green chunni spotless, as though she had not traveled miles through the dust. Pitaji looked equally pristine in his white kurta-pajama, with his blue turban perfectly symmetrical on his head. They would not be happy to see us covered in dirt, our clothes disheveled and torn. I stood up and smoothed out my salwar-kameez.

Mataji's eyes narrowed at us. "What are you bandar doing?" We kept our eyes trained on our feet.

"Chotu, Dilbagh, come with me to chop wood. Then we can till the fields." Pitaji's dark beard quivered, as though he were suppressing a laugh.

"More chores," Chotu mumbled. He reluctantly got to his feet and kicked a rock in my direction.

I opened my mouth to yell at him, but Pitaji cut in, "You must work if you wish to eat. Labor is our way of life. Honest labor is the means of our continued existence."

Dilbagh mouthed the words as they left Pitaji's mouth and Chotu laughed, but I kept quiet. Pitaji had repeated those words so many times that he had sapped them of all meaning, but it was disrespectful to mock him.

"Bhag Bhari, let's go make dinner." Mataji shifted the weight of the cloth in her arms. "We'll put this away. Tomorrow we'll make your veere new kurta-pajamas. They're growing so fast."

"Mataji, should I rub some of this on you?" I ran toward Mataji with my dirt-covered hands.

Mataji scurried away from me. "Dhoor fittay moo!" Shame on you.

After she stored the cloth bales in a basket inside the house, Mataji set a pot of daal and a jug of water next to me. I poured water into the daal to wash the lentils, and then covered the pot with my hand to strain the water. Bits of dirt and water slid out between my fingers.

Mataji placed a jug of water and a pot of wheat flour next to her. "Remember to rinse the daal again. Why do you play so rough with your veere? Your cousin Jeeti never plays that way."

Jeeti's father was my uncle, my pitaji's veer, and our families had pushed us together since we were little. I loved Jeeti—she was my closest friend—but we were different. She was the perfect kuri, and everyone in the village admired her long, shiny hair and her perfect poise. They praised her delicate embroidery, and their mouths watered at the thought of her cooking. I wasn't very good at any of that. Not that it mattered to me. I would rather wrestle in the fields, ride one of our two stately horses, or play with sticks by the creek. Jeeti's interests bored me. Still, I couldn't imagine my life without her, but I loathed it when Mataji compared us.

"Mataji, you want me to play with dolls and do kikli like a little girl? Spinning in those ridiculous circles makes me dizzy. I'd rather eat dirt."

Mataji's lips thinned in disapproval. She poured water into a mound of wheat flour and kneaded the doughy mixture. "Dhi, you are young now. Your life will change, and it will be easier for you if you behave like the other kuriyaan. What's wrong with doing kikli?" Her eyes bored into mine before she went back to pummeling the dough.

Mataji's implication irked me, just as Dilbagh's comment had earlier that day. I looked daggers at her, wishing my eyes could pierce some sense into her. "Mataji, do you remember when we went to Amritsar to see Sri Harmandir Sahib last summer?"

She raised her eyes from the roti she was flattening with a wooden rolling pin and caught my gaze. "Of course, Dhi. Such a memorable pilgrimage. You and your veere were awed to learn that your dadaji and great-uncle Langah helped build the grand gurdwara."

"That gurdwara is our holiest place of worship. You said the four entrances to the building indicated that all were welcome. And all who enter are equal. Why can't I be myself then, whether or not I am like other kuriyaan?" I rinsed the daal again.

Mataji's back tensed, and she averted her eyes. "We are all equal; this is true. As time goes by, you will understand. But at this moment, you—you must focus on the daal we are making for dinner." The expression on her face indicated that our conversation was over.

My chest tightened, and the tiny hairs on my neck prickled in frustration. Cooking daal was a talent I had no interest in perfecting.

We moved outside to make daal and rotis over the chulha. Lighting a fire inside the house led to coughing fits, so our mother preferred cooking in the fresh air. Above us, the sun was fast disappearing, making way for its sister, the moon. Mataji struck two rocks and lit a fire beneath the stove. I placed the daal pot on one side of the chulha and watched Mataji as she flipped rotis with practiced ease on the other side. A crimson glow enveloped us, expanding into the rapidly darkening night sky. For a moment, it felt like the fire that crackled underneath our humble meal burned inside me, giving me its warmth and courage.

Something hit my left arm and pulled me away from my thoughts. I turned to see a ripe mango split open on the ground next to me. Rubbing my sore arm, I scooped up the sweet treat, when I heard Chotu giggling from a tree branch above me.

"Oy, bandar, get down!"

"What? I'm not a monkey! You like mangoes, so I gifted you one. I can't help it if you don't appreciate the method of delivery," he said, landing with a thud.

I decided to let it go and peeled the skin off the juicy fruit.

Just then, Dilbagh joined us, carrying bundles of hay for our horses. They were sleek beauties, with muscles that rolled underneath their supple coats, their heads crowned with shiny manes. The horses happily lowered their muzzles to feast. Pitaji had named our horses for their animal counterparts in speed. Sher was a lion, while Kachu was a turtle. Kachu was my favorite. She was slow and obstinate but dependable, and I loved her for it.

Pitaji laid down his axe, and the five of us sat down to eat. Mataji looked pointedly at me, so I set down my mango and got up to help her. We placed plates with hot roti and daal in front of my veere and pitaji before making plates for ourselves.

In my haste, I dropped the plate in front of Chotu, and a few drops of daal splashed on his leg.

"Bhenji, you almost burned me!"

"Get your own plate next time, then," I retorted, rubbing my still-sore arm.

"We don't farm our fields all day so that food can be thrown about. People are hungry on the battlefield. Remember that when you enjoy this hot meal," said Pitaji, and his stern voice quieted our fight.

I wondered for a moment if Pitaji had ever gone hungry as a soldier, but I didn't ask. We'd already annoyed him, and there was no sense in bringing up sore topics. Even if I did, he would say he didn't recognize any pain in the service of the Guru. Sikhism was about service in adherence to dharam, duty. Yet, I wondered how you could ignore the pangs of hunger for long.

"This summer's harvest has been plentiful, the best in many summers. An abundant gift from the monsoon rains," Mataji remarked, beaming as she scooped up daal with her roti.

"The mangoes and guavas are juicy this season. I devour them in bunches," said Chotu as he shoved a bite into his mouth.

"I am happy you enjoy the fruits, but you mustn't be gluttonous, Puttar. We have to ration our food so there is enough for all," Mataji gently chided Chotu.

After that, we ate in silence under the moonlight, watching the embers from our stove's fading fire twirl in a fiery dance, twinkling like stars before cascading to the ground. I glanced up at my parents' ember-lit faces, the labors of the day reflected in the deep creases around their eyes. Dilbagh ate slow, steady, and quiet. Chotu barely took a breath between bites, and food streaked down his cheeks and chin.

"You eat like a wild animal." I laughed at Chotu, and he flicked a bite at me. I opened my mouth and caught the edible projectile in my mouth, chomping in victory.

"Chotu, don't throw anything at Bhag Bhari. I just talked about not wasting food. And Bhag Bhari, why do you continue to trouble your veer?" said Pitaji, frowning. "Your mataji makes me hot rotis every morning. And I pluck jamun for her from the trees because they are her favorite. This is the meaning of family."

Mataji nodded in agreement. "Bachche, by Waheguru's grace, our family is here, together. After the brutal murder of our ninth Guru, many of the men of our community are away fighting. Many have since lost their lives. Our women are farming the fields and fending for themselves. Remember this when you tease each other."

An image of our neighbor laboring alone in the fields came to mind, and guilt swallowed me whole, like a snake a mouse. For all the times Mataji said guilt was a useless emotion, my parents didn't hesitate to dole it out to my veere and me. Beyond the stories of distant battles, we'd been untouched by war, and the feeling of this guilt felt foreign to us children. We would feel terrible for a moment and soon forget. Perhaps this was why my parents kept repeating themselves.

After dinner, I was tasked with fetching water from the well to wash the dirty dishes. Usually, Mataji and I cleaned up after dinner, but that evening, she was helping my father sort and store produce he had brought in from the fields.

Chotu appeared and offered to help haul the pail.

"You can learn to wash dishes. I'll teach you," I said. We linked arms and walked together to the well, where I handed him the pail of water. Chotu almost fell backward trying to balance its weight. He then puffed out his chest and pretended to be strong, but his arms were trembling. I gripped the handle with him, and we ambled to the chulha in front of our house and scooped up the ash.

"Rub the plates with ash, like this, Chotu."

I demonstrated scrubbing the pots to remove the dried food, and Chotu faithfully copied my actions, vigorously working with a wet rag.

"See, Veer. You did well."

"I can understand that some tasks need muscle power and are better left to men, but anyone can clean or cook," said Chotu as he tackled the more tenacious bits on his plate.

"True, but a woman can also develop physical strength."

"As long as we finish our chores, it doesn't matter who does what," added Chotu, triumphantly raising a clean plate in the air. I smiled at my younger brother. For all his mischief, he was a wise soul.

Dilbagh was snoozing on a manji in the courtyard. We could hear his heavy breathing and guessed that he was tired. He'd risen before sunrise and helped Pitaji in the fields. He also practiced his sword-fighting skills with our father, after which he had to feed and care for the animals. He worked hard, and I secretly wondered if I had that kind of strength in me.

Beyond the sleeping form of my brother, I could see our brick home. It was large enough to be divided into three rooms—a private room for my parents, a shared one for us siblings, and one room that served as a pantry. My father's paternal uncle was a revenue official who oversaw the collection of taxes from eighty-four villages. My great-uncle and his brother, my dadaji, constructed our home, a grand house for our village. Great-Uncle Langah had also been appointed as an army commander under the sixth Guru. Under his command, Pitaji trained in shastar vidya and fought against the emperor's soldiers.

I wondered when my brothers would go to war. Dilbagh would make a good soldier, principled and dutiful, but Chotu . . . Chotu thought fighting tyranny was ridiculous.

"My arms hurt." Chotu's cheeks were streaked with ash. I could pretend not to have noticed, and he would wake up looking like a mess. But I looked at his sweet, round face and thought about him going to battle and softened.

"Clean your face before you fall asleep, little gadhe," I said, playfully pinching his arm. He grunted at me.

"Goodnight, Veer." My voice caught in my throat, and I pretended to cough. He smiled at me and rinsed his face before easing into his spot next to Dilbagh.

I stretched out on a third cot, still damp from rain earlier in the day. The field to my right stretched before me like a great sea of green, with grass stalks gently waving in the breeze. Above me, the moon hung low in a starless sky, its silvery light casting a soft glow over our village.

Unable to sleep, I mulled over the events of the day. My duty as a girl was to care for my family at home, keeping everyone well-fed and happy. But shouldn't I feel drawn to these tasks—cooking and cleaning—if they were my purpose in life? Jeeti loved to cook and stitch, and my veere seemed content tending the fields and learning to fight. They were as they should be, while I was pretending to enjoy things I didn't. Why did behaving like the other kuriyaan in the village feel so unnatural? What was wrong with me?

I thought of Pitaji fighting alongside our sixth Guru and about the soldiers starving at the battlefront. I remembered some of the stories I had heard growing up from my dadaji and his brother, my great-uncle Langah—the atrocities they had seen, the torture they had endured. But hunger. I had never really thought about dying that way.

Dilbagh's wooden practice sword lay on the ground next to him. A thrill flashed through me at the thought of sneaking into Pitaji's stash of weapons and holding his sword. I imagined gripping a kirpan and maneuvering it to knock a weapon out of an opponent's hand. A shiver of excitement ran up my spine.

Soon, the swaying crops and gentle hum of insects lulled me to sleep. My heart spun dreams wrapped in golden thread, intangible as wishes, yet as real as the rocks and soil of our land. A winding path ended at a door, beckoning me to enter, and I danced into a future that called my wandering soul.

Dreams of becoming a warrior.

Dreams of fighting for justice.

Dreams of peace.

# TWO

The crisp morning sun pressed its warmth against my cheeks. A soft hand stroked my hair.

"Dhi," Mataji spoke in a quiet voice, "I need you to make a trade at the bazaar. Chotu will come with you."

I opened my sleep-heavy eyelids and squinted at the rising sun before turning my attention to her. Mataji smiled at me, and it filled me with love.

Mataji wore a parrot-green cotton salwar-kameez. The sides of her tight hair bun were streaked with silver—she looked regal. It was as though her beautiful dark brown hair were transforming into a shiny, precious metal. How valuable that head of hair would be when it fully changed color, voicing in silence the wisdom of her life! Her oval face was still flushed from the heat of the chulha, and her skin smelled of ghee. She would smear the remnants of a pot of clarified butter on her face and lips to protect them from the dry summer heat.

"What are you looking at?" Mataji asked.

"You." I snuggled into her warmth. "What do you need from the bazaar?"

She stroked my hair again and massaged my scalp. "Trade some of our vegetables for jute rope. We need to repair the weave on the frayed manji. Ask Jeeti to help you carry things."

"Yes, Mataji."

Green jute plants grew tall in the fields during the monsoon season. Jute farmers would harvest, defoliate, and then soak the stems in water to allow everything to rot away, leaving behind the plant fibers. These fibers were then spun into coarse, strong threads and braided into rope. Traveling merchants would bring these ropes to our local bazaar to trade for produce or other goods.

"Did I hear my name?" Jeeti called out as she walked toward us.

"Where did you come from?" I asked, surprised to see her when we'd only just spoken about her.

"I came to see you. Why are you sleeping so late?" My cousin's skin was rosy from her brisk walk, and her long, silky hair was fastened in a single braid that slapped her back as she glided toward us like a majestic peacock.

"I usually rise before the sun each day, probably earlier than you . . . but I slept late last night and was lost in a sea of dreams." I averted my gaze so she wouldn't pry.

Jeeti scrunched her nose in curiosity. "What sort of dreams?"

"Teinu ki." Mind your own business.

Jeeti opened her mouth to press me for more details, but Mataji stood up and gave my cousin a tight squeeze. "Jeeti Dhi, accompany Bhag Bhari to the bazaar. Chotu will be with you. I've placed vegetables in baskets by the chulha."

I walked to the well and splashed freshly drawn water on my face from a bucket. Picking up a short daatun, a twig from a peepul tree, I walked back over to Jeeti, who was tapping her foot impatiently.

With exaggerated slowness, I used the twig's pointed end to pick pieces of food out of my teeth. Jeeti's brow furrowed. "Bhen! Be quick, or the sun will be high in the sky by the time we leave."

"I like the heat," I lied. "Jeeti, you comb your hair till it flows like silk. Why are you hurrying me, Empress?" Both Jeeti and my mataji clucked in disapproval.

I picked up my pace, chewing on the other end of the twig until it was frayed, and then rubbed the tasteless bark fibers against my teeth. Morning ritual complete, I flicked the mutilated daatun aside. Jeeti widened her eyes in disgust.

"Shall we go?" I chuckled.

We covered our heads with our chunnis. Jeeti flashed me an irritated look as we each scooped up one basket of eggplant. We balanced them on our heads and walked toward the market.

"I will be first to reach the bazaar," declared Chotu, appearing out of nowhere. He skipped ahead of us.

"Since we are going to the market, I want to see if there are any pretty fabrics I can use to stitch a new salwar-kameez set for myself." Jeeti's eyes brightened as she shifted the basket on her head.

We passed a thicket of bushes named sada-suhagan, or ever-in-marital-bliss, because the plants bloomed in all seasons. "Did you bring a trade?" I asked her.

"No, Pitaji gave me this," Jeeti replied, retrieving a single gold mohar from her satchel. "He said I shouldn't tell Mataji, and that I could use it to buy something special."

I stared at the shiny coin, enamored of the fortune she was carrying. My parents didn't believe in gifting mohars to us, a prize they reserved for extraordinary achievements. Pride silenced me from asking her what she had done to deserve one. I kicked a tiny pebble down the dirt road, and Jeeti followed suit.

"I am starving. Mataji sent me off before I could eat," I complained, feeling more irritated than I knew I should. People were starving on the battlefront.

"There's a mango tree." Jeeti gestured awkwardly with her basket-topped head.

"Chotu, wait!" I set my basket down and shimmied up the tree trunk to pluck mangoes for us. I threw one at Jeeti before I wiggled back down. She attempted to catch it but missed, and the fruit landed at her feet.

Jeeti picked it up and squeezed it. "How do you climb trees so quickly? It must be because you are taller and stronger than I am."

"It's practice," I laughed. "And hunger."

The annoyance I felt earlier melted away. It was true I did not have a mohar, but I could pluck fruit from the highest trees.

We sucked on our saffron-yellow mangoes, sweet as honey, licking our fingers as we arrived at the market. The bazaar was busier than a beehive and smelled of incense, wet earth, and sweat. The din of bargaining enveloped us as we took in the scene. Merchants crowded closely together in a field. There were fruits and vegetables on display alongside muslin, buffalo hide, and shiny churriyaan, or bangles, sparkling in the sunlight. More sellers were making their way through the slow-moving crowds. They carried baskets of wares on their heads or towed small wagons piled with goods.

We wandered the narrow lanes between stalls, when Jeeti stopped to watch an amber-eyed seller lay colorful fabric atop her merchant rug. The woman sported a bright purple headscarf over her curly hair and was putting on quite a show. A small crowd gathered around her, their eyes bright with excitement.

"Those fabrics look amazing, no?" Jeeti stood there, her jaw slack and her face aglow with interest.

I nodded, feigning interest. Chotu picked his nails behind us. My eyes drifted to three boys roughhousing behind the stall. The basket of eggplant felt like a load of bricks on my head.

"You may not be interested, but I am looking to buy fabric," said Jeeti. She shifted her basket and took half a step closer to admire the material.

"Can we trade for jute, please? That is why we are here, and this basket is heavy." I shifted the basket, which provided little relief.

"I thought you were strong, bandari," Jeeti teased.

"I am willing to exchange these two milk pails for that red fabric," a woman bargained with the seller.

"Do you know how difficult it is to harvest, spin, and

weave this cotton? Much harder than milking cows." The fabric merchant scolded her potential customer with her eyes.

"Do you know how heavy two pails of milk are? I carried them all the way here," the customer scoffed, and turned away. She bumped into Jeeti, who had moved in behind her. I raised my hand to steady Jeeti's basket.

The seller turned her attention to us, and a coy smile brightened her face. Jeeti's back straightened, and her expression changed. She didn't trust the seller.

"If you give me both those baskets of vegetables, you may have a bale of this fabric. Choose your color." The woman whipped out a yellow cloth, then an emerald-green one, and then a rich brown one, creating a cloud of color around us.

"These aren't of very good quality. We are here for jute, not for these cheap fabrics," said Jeeti, trying to sound aloof.

"They are of the highest quality. We make the fabrics far from here, so we also have to pay for our travels. And we are afraid to make these long journeys during this tumultuous time." The traveler spoke as though she were singing a melody. "We are not mighty warriors like you Sikhs, still resisting the forces from Delhi."

Jeeti ignored her and stomped away. I quickened my pace to keep up with her through the jostling crowds. Chotu shuffled behind us.

"I thought you wanted to look at fabric. Did you think it wasn't good?" I asked, but Jeeti didn't reply. "Was the seller's offer unfair? It sounded like fabric-making is strenuous, and then if they travel long distances in wartime to trade . . ." I trailed off. "You didn't offer your mohar, kanjus." I pinched Jeeti's arm.

"Oy, Bhen! I am not cheap. These sellers are known to be swindlers. And to talk about us Sikhs when we are most at risk. We have no wealth to offer Aurangzeb as taxes like the hill kings do. Chee, that traveler's complaint was more bitter than karela," said Jeeti in a condescending tone, as though she were more worldly than us. Yet, we had both lived in the same village our entire lives.

"Ha, we may not have wealth for taxes, but maybe these sellers don't either. And we are mighty warriors. The seller did us no harm. Instead of blaming one another, why don't we think about how we can help each other in times of trouble?" I said.

I felt momentarily at a loss for words. A waft of smoke brought back a fond memory. "Maybe you are right. I don't come to the bazaar much, except when the blacksmiths are selling swords. And even then, I don't always get to see them in action unless Pitaji takes me along." I relished the smell of metal and leather and the sight of row upon row of finely crafted blades. Someday I wanted to find a way to trade for a weapon of my own. "If you believe the sellers to be dishonest, then why trade for their wares?"

"Who else should we trade with? The royal empire for gems and gold?" Sarcasm dripped from her mouth like sugarcane juice. "We are not privileged. And not everything we need grows on trees."

"Now you sound more bitter than karela."

"Can we finish our trade and go home?" said Chotu, his face suffused with boredom.

"Yes." Jeeti spun around, nearly losing the top layer of eggplant from her basket, and moved on.

We continued our quest to find the jute seller. Jeeti brushed shoulders with a man, and a vegetable fell out of her basket. I freed up one hand and caught it just before it hit the ground.

Just then, a woman screamed at a merchant who stretched a cloth taut. "Stop, ullu ka patha!" Son of an owl. "You are ripping the cloth in half." I glanced at the merchant, who did appear to be stretching the cloth to make the most of its measure.

Finally, we arrived at the jute merchant. The man's body was rope-thin, his arms twiglike. His black mustache curled upward to touch the tip of his nose, and his creased cheeks hung like buffalo hide, marking him a faithful devotee of the sun.

"May we trade these vegetables for a fair amount of jute?" I asked, as my mataji had taught me. Chotu raised his eyebrow at my bartering skills, and I elbowed him in case he decided to giggle. The man nodded gleefully. He dumped the produce out of our baskets onto a mat and reloaded our containers with more jute than I thought fair. I nodded in gratitude as we walked away.

"He was a seller," I said to Jeeti, just to get a rise out of her, "but he seemed honest, even generous."

"Yes, but you were lucky today," she retorted and strode off in a huff.

When we returned home, we set the jute-filled baskets down by Mataji. She was squatting near the chulha, sweeping out the ashes.

"Where is everyone?" I asked.

"Your pitaji is in the fields, and Dilbagh is playing with friends. He will be back soon."

Mal akharas—he'd be wrestling or playing gilli-danda, my favorite puck-and-stick sport. I'd carried heavy baskets from the bazaar while my veer played games. *Seemed fair.* Before Mataji could assign me more chores, I yanked Jeeti's hand and pulled her to where I knew Dilbagh would be. Chotu scurried after us.

"Oy! Come back soon! And Jeeti, make sure she doesn't wrestle with the boys," Mataji yelled after us, but we were already halfway through the fields and too far to respond.

We burst into a dirt clearing dotted with clumps of grass, panting and huffing. I held on to my knees, trying to catch my breath. My temples were moist with perspiration. Jeeti spotted a few of the village kuriyaan playing with marbles and plopped down on the ground next to them.

"Next time, don't make me run so fast," panted Jeeti, as she shook the marbles in her hand for emphasis.

"Lazy," I teased, smiling.

Chotu and I left her and walked toward the nearby jamun tree, where a group of boys were wrestling each other. Dilbagh was getting ready to take on another boy from the village.

My cousin Gurdas was squatting beneath the tree, popping dark purple jamun berries into his mouth and sucking in his cheeks at their tart taste. Gurdas's pitaji was my mataji's brother—my mamaji. Gurdas was a few years older than us. He also had a sister, Jasmeet, who was several years younger than us. Mataji once said she saw the beginnings of a swollen belly on Mamiji two times between Gurdas's and Jasmeet's births, but no baby was ever born. It must have been painful for my mamiji to lose an unborn baby, and Jasmeet was understandably Mamiji's favorite child.

Gurdas walked over to my side. "Bhen, who do you think will win this match?"

"That brute ox, Kulwinder," I said, surprising myself with my meanness. Kulwinder was the biggest boy in our village.

Gurdas snorted, and a jamun flew out of his mouth. "I won't tell Dilbagh that you don't believe in him."

"He doesn't appreciate his privilege in this world, unlike some others. He doesn't want to win bad enough." I glanced at Gurdas, then quickly looked away.

"Others like who?" asked Gurdas, but I didn't respond. My cousin returned to sit under the tree with Chotu.

Dilbagh and Kulwinder held out their arms with their feet spread wide as they circled one another, preparing to wrestle. Kulwinder made the first move. He grabbed Dilbagh's hair and threw him to the ground. He moved to jump on top of Dilbagh and claim victory, but my brother put his leg up just as his opponent pounced. The kick sent him flailing backward. They both jumped up, and Kulwinder put his hands around Dilbagh's throat and tried to strangle him. Dilbagh's face reddened as he yanked at the boy's hands and tried to pull away. But Kulwinder wouldn't stop. I held my breath. *Don't panic.* Chotu's eyes widened in fear, and he rushed to my side.

"Chaaaaa!"

I snapped out of my trance and ran toward Dilbagh. I threw the weight of my body against Kulwinder and knocked him off my veer. Kulwinder let go and sneered at me.

"Are you trying to kill Dilbagh?" I demanded, my face flushed from a mix of anger and exertion.

"I would have let him go." Kulwinder shrugged.

Dilbagh rubbed his throat as he tried to catch his breath. "Bhenji, why are you watching the match? Please go play with Jeeti."

I had embarrassed him. No boy wanted his bhen defending him. "I saved your life, and you are pushing me away?"

"Your bhen wants to wrestle me," Kulwinder scoffed.

The kuriyaan playing with marbles nearby muffled their giggles with their hands. I stared long and hard at the leader of the pack, and fear flickered across her face. I'd silenced her with my eyes. I turned and looked back at Kulwinder's smug face. Filled with rage, I charged at him, my fury giving me momentum, and the biggest boy in the village fell to the ground. I wanted to kick dirt in his face, but I heard Chotu cheering and stopped myself.

"Bhenji, you knocked down Kulwinder. Bravo!" Chotu whistled and clapped.

Dilbagh covered Chotu's mouth and spoke to me in a low voice. "Bhenji, go home now." *My younger brother was telling me what to do?*

"No," I snapped. Dilbagh glared at me, but I wasn't going to let him have his way.

Kulwinder rose and dusted himself off. "Very few people can knock me down. My great-dadaji learned mal akharas from the source himself, our second Guru."

"Then why aren't you more skilled at wrestling?" My words tasted like fire in my mouth.

His thick brow furrowed. "Show me how well you wrestle, then. I'll let you have the first move."

"You'll regret it," I sneered.

"Bhenji, stop," begged Dilbagh, but neither Kulwinder nor I were listening.

We circled each other. Kulwinder's trunk-like legs and heavy footfalls sent puffs of dirt up into the air with each step he took. He stood a head taller than me, and he was much broader at the shoulders. I caught a glimpse of Dilbagh to my right, rooted to his spot with his arms crossed. Chotu sat on the ground next to him and beamed with excitement, jamun juice dribbling down his chin.

In one swift move, I placed my hands on Kulwinder's shoulders and struck him in his stomach with my knee. He clutched his stomach for a moment and then punched me in the chest and stomach. The double strike sucked the air out of me. He was much stronger than anyone I had fought before—certainly stronger than my veere. I fell to my knees, hands on the gravel, steadying myself. My long hair unraveled beneath my chunni and almost touched the ground. I took a deep breath, but it felt like no amount of air would ever be enough.

I jumped back to my feet, still heaving. Kulwinder charged at me. I gripped his hair and attempted to shake him. It was an unwise move, because he was far too heavy. He ripped my hands off his head and threw a punch toward my right cheek. But he was slow, so I was able to duck, and he ended up slugging the air. I jumped up and used both my fists to strike his head. The blow made him dizzy, and seeing my opening, I wrestled him to the ground. With the beast on the ground, I placed my foot on his stomach to signify victory. My heart thumped in my chest, and my fist still longed to plow into Kulwinder's sizable gut.

Chotu raced toward me and shouted in triumph, "Jit gaye!" You won!

Jeeti had joined the crowd of spectators by then. She hugged me, but her eyes chided me for doing exactly what Mataji had told me not to do. Chotu did a little dance before he threw his arms around me. My cousin Gurdas, still seated beneath the tree, smiled at me. A flicker of pride flashed across his face. I spun in circles, hands to the sky, and basked in jubilation for one glorious moment.

That's when I noticed Dilbagh walking back toward our home, and my stomach sank. I was going to be in trouble.

Back home, Mataji hovered over the large wooden frame of a cot. Her hand bobbed up and down as she wove jute rope to create a mesh in the center of the manji. She glanced up at us as we approached and took in my dirt-encrusted clothes and disheveled hair.

Jeeti shifted uncomfortably. "I am going home, Bhen."

"Mataji, we were—" I began.

"Dilbagh already told me what happened. Tomorrow is a remembrance of our fifth and ninth Gurus' martyrdom. The village will be preparing a meal, langar, in their honor in front of our home. I expect you to rise early to help with the cooking," she said, her tone flat. The disappointment in her voice stung.

# THREE

The next morning, I squatted beside Mataji in a group of aunties making roti pede under the warm sun.

I was wearing my mataji's hand-stitched, mango-yellow salwar-kameez. My mother knew I only cared about how comfortable the clothing was. Still, she managed to sneak in subtle beadwork on the kameez, adding a matching border on the chunni and salwar. I had to admit, the outfit looked elegant. I draped the chunni over the top of my head, but it kept sliding down the back and pooling around my neck. Constantly adjusting the chunni to cover my hair vexed me. I wanted to concentrate on making the balls of dough, not fixing my uncooperative clothes. My hair bun wasn't holding the chunni up, contrary to Mataji's insistence that it would. Usually, I would wear my hair in one or two braids, with my chunni carelessly flung over my shoulders. But in front of the community, I had to look respectable and cover my head. I understood this, but it was still an annoyance.

I glanced at the older woman on my right, who, despite her stoic expression, was beautiful. She had warm eyes that creased at the corners, an aquiline nose, and cheekbones shaped like jamun high up on her face.

"Aunty, you are so good at making perfectly round pede," I said.

She smiled at me warmly. "When you are as old as me, you too will excel at pede making."

I smiled and pretended to take it as a compliment. I wasn't going to spend my life rolling out roti pede.

As I pulled out tiny sections of the dough to roll them, a neighbor in a saffron-colored salwar-kameez watched me. "Dhi, your pede are too small," she said. She dipped her hand into a large clay pot and handed me an extra wad of dough to fatten up my creations.

"No, no, they are too big," her round-faced friend countered and yanked the extra dough back.

Mataji gave me a sideways smirk and a pat on my hand to indicate my pede were fine. She rolled the balls out into flat circles, which would soon be cooked to perfection over the chulha.

A yellow-toothed aunty took it upon herself to share a history lesson with me. "Dhi, do you know how Guru Gobind Singh Ji became our tenth guru at the age of eight? It was after his pitaji, who bore witness to the cruelty of the emperor, was beheaded many seasons ago."

I nodded because Mataji had told me the story. The ninth Guru was the same age as my father when his light merged with the Light. If anything happened to my pitaji, the pain would be unbearable.

Everyone imagines that people cry uncontrollably when a loved one dies. But that was not what I had seen. Instead, quiet tears were shed and quickly wiped away, perhaps because we were in a war. Our people seemed to be numb, or maybe they pretended to be numb to protect themselves. When warriors died, their families were sad and proud all at once.

I forgot to dip my hand in dry flour every so often, so I would pause to rub the sticky dough off my palms. As I scrubbed, my peda critics exchanged whispers. They peered at the solemn-looking aunty next to me, who seemed lost in her thoughts.

"Satwinder . . . not just her husband, but both sons too. Under the sixth Guru . . . sad, but dutiful in the service of the Guru . . . She lives with her dhi now . . ." They covered the sides of their mouths as they gossiped. I disliked the way the women talked about her, and I wanted to ease her pain. But what could I say or do to comfort a mother who lost her children?

We sat in silence for several minutes, when Satwinder Aunty turned to look at me. I smiled at her when our eyes met. She seemed comforted by my presence. "The men in my family died with honor, but . . . but I don't know if he was hungry before he died." I wasn't sure whom she was talking about, but I was afraid to interrupt.

"Can you believe that is what I think about when my thoughts drift to my younger puttar, my son? Mani had a ravenous appetite, but food supplies at the battlefield were limited, so I don't know if he died hungry." She rolled the dough between her palms and set it down. She stared at the ball for a moment and began to weep. Her whole body shook, and she wrapped her arms around herself.

I threw my arms around her and squeezed her tight until the shaking subsided. If grief is a measure of your love, then Satwinder Aunty's love for her puttar was boundless. How many other matajis were suffering like her?

Autumn arrived buoyantly in my fourteenth year. And though the seasons changed, we did not. One evening my veere and I were wrestling, the boys teaming up since neither could beat me on their own, when our cousin Gurdas appeared. Seeing us, his eyebrows drew close, and he charged in our direction. He thrust his strong shoulders forward to intimidate my veere. Dilbagh and Chotu wriggled free of my grip and darted toward home, squelching in mud as they ran.

I dusted the leaves and dirt off and went to draw water from the well to wash the dirty laundry I had abandoned earlier. Gurdas sat next to me while I squished clothes into the pail to soak them. I glanced at him. The sprouts of hair on his chin and cheeks had grown into a beard; he was beginning to look like a man. *When will he be sent off to war?*

"It's good to see you, Veerji." I scrubbed the clothes vigorously. "Thank you for scaring off my veere. Mataji has made subji and roti if you're hungry."

"I am, because I love your mataji's cooking." Gurdas hugged my shoulders since my hands were busy. "But, that is not why I came, Bhen. I am older now, so men in the community talk to me about the state of affairs in Hindustan."

"What are you talking about? What state of affairs? News about the emperor and the hill kings scheming is nothing new."

"Your parents don't tell you much because they love you. I don't mean to frighten you, dear sister, but we are not safe. Sikhs are now considered a threat to the throne in Delhi. If the emperor's soldiers or any of the hill kings launch an attack here in Jhabal Kalan, our village will be wiped out."

A shiver ran up my spine. I took my hands out of the water and wiped them on the sides of my salwar. "Why would the emperor's soldiers come here?"

"We cannot predict where their next attack will be. You must be able to fend for yourself should anyone decide to launch an offensive against our home. You're my choti bhen, and if you or the family are harmed, I would hate myself for not teaching you to defend yourself. Especially because I know you are capable of fighting."

Gurdas's love felt like home. After Jeeti, he was my closest cousin and my guiding star. In turn, my younger veere looked to me for guidance. That's how it was with our families—the older siblings and cousins took care of the younger ones.

"Are you offering to train me for battle, Veerji?" I asked in disbelief.

"Your natural skills as a warrior are no secret. I am still learning shastar vidya, but I want to teach you what I know—in secret," he whispered. "This way, you can protect our families if we are attacked. But we must be careful not to be seen. My pitaji would never forgive me. Neither would yours."

I jumped up in joy and twirled around, when I probably should have been fearful. "Truly, Veerji—?"

"Chup, be quiet. After the adults are asleep, we will meet at the far edge of the fields and practice under the moonlight. You must be careful." He got up and went inside.

His father, my mamaji, walked over carrying some mangoes. "Washing clothes?"

I nodded and returned to my work. "Gurdas Veer is inside." I pointed toward the house. "And Jasmeet is probably on the other side, swinging from trees with Chotu."

Mamaji squatted next to me and handed me a ripe mango. "I saved the sweetest one for you." I pressed the yellow skin of the fruit, and to my satisfaction, it squished inward just a little bit.

"You remember how the wheat looks in our fields, Dhi?" he asked.

"Of course."

"All that wheat looks the same from afar. But if you look closely, you'll see the wheat ears are not exactly alike. Some are longer, some shorter, some thicker, and some skinnier. All different, but all good to eat." Mamaji smiled at me warmly.

What was he implying? Did he know of my longing to be a warrior? I smiled at my mamaji, and he leaned forward to pat my head gently. My earliest memories of my uncle were of him affectionately stroking my hair. Tears streamed down my cheeks, and Mamaji wiped them away.

"Why are you crying?"

"I want to protect my family. I know we are not safe here." Gurdas's words echoed in my mind.

"Dhi, tell me, who is safe at all times? When it is our time to go, it is our time to go. And how can we complain about joining Waheguru? Suffering is only in this world, not there," he said, pointing to the sky.

Mamaji looked away, lost in thought. Then his jaw dropped. His eyebrows came together, as though he suddenly understood the meaning of my words. "Dhi, you will not be the one to fight these battles. When I said each wheat ear is different, I didn't mean . . . You may be unique, but that does not mean you are fit for war. Is that what you thought?" He paused, but when I didn't respond, he continued, "You are the eldest dhi, and your dharam is to care for this family and your family to come. Do you understand that?"

I looked away, unable to meet his gaze, unable to answer his questions. How absurd my fantasies were. Mamaji's love for me was pure, so there had to be something wrong with me. Why couldn't I shake off this feeling, this call to battle? I relished the idea of my cousin teaching me to wield a sword. And yet, this was not my dharam. Why did my heart pull me in opposite directions?

Chotu walked over, interrupting my thoughts. He was carrying a giggling Jasmeet upside down, and she was squirming and pretending to escape from his clutches.

"This bandar has been hanging from a tree branch. It's time to come down," said Chotu as he flipped her over and set her down. She steadied herself before running to her pitaji and throwing her arms around him.

"Let's go home, bachche. Sat Sri Akal." Mamaji pressed his palms together and set off with Jasmeet in tow.

That evening, it felt like the sun would never set. I imagined the weight of a sword in my hand. Would we practice with a real kirpan? I pictured myself swinging it and shocking my cousin by deftly knocking his weapon from his hands.

Mataji watched me as I rushed through my chores. "Bhag Bhari, the pots are still crusted with dry subji at the bottom. Get a handful of ashes from the chulha and scrub them again."

"Sorry, Mataji. I'll do them again." I was annoyed at having to redo my meaningless work, but I couldn't stop smiling. Dishes or not, I was going to be a warrior. I scooped ashes up from beneath the stove and squatted to scrub the pot hastily.

Mataji paused her mending. "Why are you acting so strange?"

"No reason." I left her side and headed to the well to fetch some water.

Long after sunset, I retreated to my manji under the watchful gaze of a yellow moon. Dilbagh snored like thunder. I lay still, counting his loud breathing until it was the only sound I could hear. Inside, Mataji, Pitaji, and Chotu were fast asleep. Once I was sure it was safe to leave home, I tiptoed toward the edge of the field. Crossing the border, I was certain that no one could hear me, and I began walking at my regular pace.

Gurdas's silhouette took shape in the distance. I moved to join him, and as soon as he saw me, my cousin threw a weapon at me.

"Ahhh!" Startled, I jumped, and the sword fell to the ground. "Are you trying to kill me?"

"It is a wooden sword. I carved these for our practice sessions. It is dark, and I don't want us to hurt each other with real swords if we can't see very well. I brought a real kirpan, which you can handle to feel its weight, but we will practice with these wooden ones."

I picked up the wooden weapon and rubbed my palm over its surface. "It's well made. How long did this take you?"

"It took time, but I didn't mind working on it. Now that you have your sword, I'll show you a few basic skills. We won't practice with other weapons, but if someone attacks you, you will have mastered some basic self-defense moves," explained Gurdas, sounding like my mother giving me a sewing lesson. I wanted to laugh, but this was too important an opportunity to ruin with an ill-timed giggle.

An errant breeze blew past us and sent a shiver of excitement up my spine.

"Bhen, first we position ourselves. Face me with your hips pointing forward. Place your left foot ahead of your right foot and keep your feet in line with your shoulders." Gurdas demonstrated the stance and then positioned himself in front of me.

Our eyes met in anticipation. Now nervous, I shuffled my left foot in front of my right. Gurdas dropped down and gripped my right ankle. He moved my foot out to widen my stance, then stood up and faced me again.

He patted the hilt of his wooden sword. "Grip this part firmly but with ease. Keep your fingers spread apart as you hold it. Have confidence in your hold."

I nodded. "I am a natural, remember."

"Arrogance is the enemy of skill, while practice is your friend. Now, hold your sword up toward your right side with both hands at shoulder level." Chastised, I followed the directions with humility. Gurdas then repositioned my left hand to place it below my right.

He held up his weapon in the same way and nodded at me. "We will start with your move. Lean your sword forward in anticipation of any movement. At the same time, step forward and slide to your right. This will move you out of my line of attack. Let me show you how." Gurdas moved in beside me. He swung his sword forward and stepped to the right, keeping his left foot planted.

"Can you practice this move, Bhen?"

I swung my sword and stepped forward, but my balance wavered. Gurdas steadied me. "Good try. However, you look uncomfortable, as though your stance is too wide. You are smaller, so don't take as wide a step as I did. Make moves guided by your own body. You must always be aware of your physical capabilities and constraints."

"Can you show me once more?" I asked, and Gurdas obliged. I practiced the move three more times. The first time, my balance was all wrong, and I fell. The second time, I slashed the air with my sword and dropped it. *Focus. This is your opportunity to learn.* Finally, on the third try, I controlled my sword's movement correctly and ended the move in a position that felt natural. Gurdas nodded in approval.

He stepped away from me. "Now, for the counter-attack." I squinted my eyes to focus on his dark form.

"When you bring your sword down toward my left shoulder, I will step forward with my right foot and use my sword against yours, countering your attack." Gurdas demonstrated this a few times.

"Are you ready?" he asked.

"Yes." I straightened my back.

We stood facing one another again, and I held my sword in the way my cousin showed me. We nodded at one another, indicating our readiness. I brought my sword down in a straight line toward his shoulder and stepped forward to my right. Gurdas stepped forward with his right foot and wielded his sword against mine to counter. Surprised by the force of his attack, I dropped my sword.

I recovered and attacked again, but he quickly blocked me, and I fell in the process. Embarrassed, I jumped up and dusted my clothes. We practiced this sequence twice and then switched roles. We finally found our rhythm, and our swords clashed time and again. I felt at ease with my cousin, and we moved like dancers in a moonlight performance.

"Well done!" exclaimed Gurdas. "You took your time to learn the moves, but your execution was natural. I knew you'd be a fast learner."

I could feel my face reddening. My ears ringing with praise, I failed to see his final attack coming. I raised my sword too late, and he struck me in the chest. I abruptly retreated, not from pain but a sense of failure.

"That would have been your death, Bhen." Gurdas lowered his weapon and walked to retrieve his belongings. He picked up his kirpan and drew the blade from its sheath. "It's late, and we have to rise early tomorrow. For our last lesson tonight, try holding this kirpan so you can feel its weight." Gurdas placed the sword in my extended hand.

Stunned by the weight of this exquisite weapon, my arm dropped even as I firmly gripped the hilt. It was as heavy as my pitaji's precious sword. The curved steel blade was razor-sharp, with a few tiny scratches from use. The hilt was covered with intricate designs etched into the metal.

The steel masterpiece felt cold. I shifted the weight of the sword in my hands. "It's heavy. This would be much harder to fight with than the wooden ones."

"Yes, Bhen." My cousin sounded deep and confident, like a river.

"Is this Mamaji's?" I asked, suddenly nervous. "He would not like me using it."

Gurdas's expression softened. "We cannot change anyone but ourselves."

Tears filled my eyes. "Thank you, Veerji. You'll never know what you've done for me."

Gurdas smiled. "This is only the beginning. In time, we will practice with real swords."

When I returned to the hut, Chotu sat up on a manji and stared at me. I froze.

"Where have you been? I woke up and saw you were missing. I thought you'd been abducted, but then I saw only one dusty trail of footprints, so I knew you'd sneaked off somewhere on your own," he whispered.

I knelt beside Chotu and squeezed his hand. "Please don't be angry with me. Can you keep a secret?"

"Hmph." Chotu pulled his hand from my grip and crossed his arms in front of him.

"I'm learning how to use a sword from Gurdas Veerji. He wants us to be able to defend ourselves in case our village is attacked. I don't want to alarm you, but we are not safe— even here, in Jhabal Kalan—so I must be able to fight for our family."

"You didn't think to include me?" He looked hurt.

"Pitaji trains you and Dilbagh, but you know he wouldn't teach me. If he did, Mataji would find a way to stop it by giving me chores. As you get older, our father will teach you all he knows."

"I'll keep your secret, Bhenji. But only if you take me with you."

The following day, I was woken up by Jeeti's insistent nudging. I had slept past sunrise.

"Wake up! Wake up! Why are you sleeping so late?" Jeeti demanded to know. "Let's go to the fields before we are pulled into work."

I yawned. "Is there anything to eat first? I am hungry."

"Why are you always hungry? What have you been up to?" asked Jeeti, suspicion writ large upon her face.

"Teinu ki?" I rose from the manji to grab a guava from a nearby basket.

Jeeti and I set off toward the fields. After a while, we stopped and sat beneath a banyan tree, its fallen leaves forming a yellow cushion beneath us. I shifted until I found a comfortable position, avoiding the tree roots that stuck out of the soil. Nearby, a line of ants marched up the tree trunk. I watched them for a while, squinting my eyes at the bright morning sun filtering through the canopy. A gentle breeze blew past, and I wrapped my arms around myself for warmth.

Lulled by our beautiful surroundings, I spilled my secret like a knocked-over vessel of water. "Jeeti, Gurdas is training me to wield a kirpan."

"Training you? What do you mean? Why? And what will your parents say, Bhag Bhari?"

I ignored her, consumed by my joy. "They're not going to find out."

"Why is Gurdas teaching you?" she whispered, as if someone could overhear us.

"Our people are in a war, Jeeti. We are never safe, not even in our perfect little village of Jhabal Kalan. Gurdas believes I would be a skilled warrior, and he wants me to be able to protect our families if there is an attack. You should learn, too."

Jeeti wrinkled her nose and shook her head. "Nonsense."

I ignored her and gushed on. "We used wooden swords to practice, weapons Gurdas carved. He also brought Mamaji's kirpan for me to hold. It was magnificent. He says soon we will practice with real swords, and he will teach me everything he knows."

Jeeti looked uncomfortable. "Bhen, you should not be doing this."

"I cannot allow our community to be ravaged if we are attacked. You can't tell anyone, even if you disapprove. Vaada karo. Promise me."

Jeeti's brows came together in thought as she picked at a blade of grass. "I promise not to tell anyone about last night. But you need to stop this nonsense. Soon we'll be old enough to marry, and what man wants a wife who could cut him in two?"

"The right man for me would." I picked up twigs and threw them into the air one by one. "I wish you understood me."

Jeeti nudged me and laughed. "Pagali, once you realize your place in the world, can you go back to being just a kuri?"

I playfully threw a twig at my cousin, but I was hurt. And she had planted a tiny seed of doubt. Maybe she was right. Who did I think I was, dreaming of fighting as a trained warrior?

# FOUR

Gurdas did not want to train every day and risk getting caught, so we agreed to meet seven nights after our first practice. Mataji and Pitaji had gone to sleep later than usual, which delayed my departure. Gurdas was waiting for us under a large peepul tree, its dense canopy blocking any moonlight from the night sky.

"Veerji," said Chotu, "what are you teaching us today?"

I elbowed Chotu hard. "I apologize, Veer. This little gadha caught me sneaking back after our first training session and threatened to tell our parents if he couldn't participate. So, now you have two students—one girl and one donkey."

Gurdas laughed. "What do you think I can teach you that your pitaji can't?"

Chotu shrugged. "If Bhenji is training, then so am I!"

"And Dilbagh?" Gurdas fiddled with the sword in his hand.

I exchanged a nervous glance with Chotu. "He'd never approve. Please don't tell him."

Gurdas didn't respond, and I took his silence to be an unspoken agreement. "Sword fighting requires you to be in constant motion, using your body weight as leverage." He slid his sword out of its sheath. "You two can work together as partners. But first, I am going to show you a basic chop."

Gurdas lunged forward with his left foot, keeping his right foot planted and spacing his feet two shoulder lengths apart diagonally. He then slashed his sword diagonally from above his right shoulder to just above his left knee. Our cousin then shifted his weight to lead with the right foot while simultaneously lifting his sword above his head with his left hand. He swiped the blade down to just above his right knee. He did this in the space of a breath.

"We will work on each side before combining them. It takes time to perfect this move," he advised, resuming his teacherly discourse.

Gurdas set his sword down and scooped up the two wooden swords, handing them to Chotu and me. "Stand behind me, and lunge forward with your left foot. Do not place your right foot in a straight line behind your left, or you will lose your balance." Gurdas watched us, and once he was convinced we weren't going to topple, he retrieved his weapon and repeated the move.

"Copy me."

We swiped in unison, and Chotu's stick hit his knee. Gurdas walked over and corrected his move, swinging it gracefully to land just beyond Chotu's leg. "I want you to practice this thrice on each side."

Chotu furrowed his brow as he concentrated. He looked so solemn and silly at the same time. I couldn't help it and burst out laughing. Gurdas snickered.

"What are you laughing at? You gadhe!" Chotu glowered at us. I fell to the ground clutching my stomach, while Gurdas jumped on all fours like a donkey. Chotu seethed and cursed until we stopped and resumed practice.

"Bhen, you alternate well," Gurdas praised. Hypnotized by the repetitive motion, I hadn't realized I had been switching between lunges and sword chops with fluid movements.

Gurdas stood in front of Chotu and demonstrated the move for him again. I took a break and watched Chotu. He was swinging his weapon with accuracy and positioning himself well.

I felt bad for teasing my sweet veer. "One more practice against me, Chotu?"

We positioned ourselves to attack, when we heard footsteps crunching on the grass.

"Who's there?" Gurdas swiftly slid his kirpan out of its sheath, ready to defend.

Pitaji swooped in and stood before us. "Who's there? Who's there? What do you mean, asking me 'who's there?'"

I dropped my wooden weapon, stunned. The tiny hairs on my neck stood up, and my heart skipped a beat as it pounded against my chest.

Pitaji gritted his bared teeth. "I woke up in a panic, thinking my bachche had been abducted by the emperor's soldiers, and I discover my dhi learning to fight like a man in the middle of the night."

"Pitaji—" I needed him to understand.

"No, Dhi, no. Don't say anything more! I forbid you to meet Gurdas again like this." Pitaji balled his hands into tight fists. "Gurdas, how can you call yourself a veerji if you train your bhen to die?" Pitaji stormed over to me and grabbed me by the ear to drag me home.

I was utterly humiliated. "Yes, just because I am a female, I cannot die in battle. I suppose you think a woman's life is more important than a man's!" I wasn't making much sense. I yanked myself free of Pitaji's grip, regretting the words that exploded from within. *I am shameful. I am disrespectful.*

Barely able to see through my tears, I ran as quickly as my legs would carry me. My feet thudded on the hard dirt, and my heart throbbed in rhythm inside my chest. I was sick with fear. My skin was on fire, and my clothes and hair, slick with perspiration, clung to my skin. When I got home, I threw myself onto an empty manji and gasped for air. All of this was my fault. How could I be so careless?

Pitaji didn't speak to me for three days after the incident. My heart had settled permanently in my stomach.

*I have to speak to him.*

I slowly walked across dew-laden grass to where my father was chopping wood behind our home. The cool morning air soothed my skin, but my insides were in tumult.

"Pitaji."

It was ominously silent, save for the sound of his axe striking wood. Pitaji paused and shook his arms, sore from the weight of the axe. He gripped the handle again and swung the blade with all his might into a tree trunk. His face was suffused with fury—I'd never seen him this angry. He pretended not to notice my presence. Defeated and deeply hurt, I left my hero's side.

"Mataji, shall I fetch water from the well and wash the clothes?" I'd returned to the courtyard and found my mother making rotis. She shrugged at me, her face blank.

The tension in our home was so thick that you could cut through it with a dagger. I needed to get away. Chotu and I sneaked off to the far end of our fields, where tall trees kissed the sky and the wind carried the faintly sweet smell of wheat. We gathered long sticks and used them to practice the moves Gurdas taught us. How I wished to see my cousin.

And then, as if my wish had been granted, he appeared out of nowhere.

"Chotu. Bhen." Gurdas had a long face.

"Don't worry, Veerji. Pitaji is angry now, but he will soon forget, and we can meet again," I said with as much cheer as I could muster. The sun caught my eye, and I squinted at him.

"That's not why I came." He shifted uncomfortably. "I need to let you know something. Yesterday, my father informed me that he and I have been called to Guru Gobind Singh Ji's side in Anandpur Sahib. I am of age . . . and I must fight."

My stomach sank. "What?"

"You don't have to react like that. Many warriors have returned unharmed. Look at your pitaji. And even if I don't, there is no greater privilege than dying in the service of the Guru."

"Pitaji told us it was by luck that he survived," said Chotu, looking befuddled. He dropped his gaze and fiddled with his make-believe sword instead. We understood that being called to fight was an honor, but this was too close to home.

"Chotu is right. As are you, Veerji. You must go, but we—I—want to go with you, so I can protect you and Mamaji from harm. I, too, would be honored to serve the Guru." My eyes stung as I held back tears.

"Bhen, this is my dharam, and I accept it with dignity. Our Guru needs us." Gurdas placed his hand on my arm. "You must stay here and protect our family."

"When do you leave?" My limbs were starting to feel numb.

"In five nights' time."

The following day, I felt flustered. I needed to find Jeeti. I ran to the path between our homes at the edge of our fields and called out her name.

"Jeeti!" I screamed. She rushed toward me.

We sat down. Tall, green blades of grass danced beneath an enormous turquoise sky. Their soft rustling was the sound of peace and joy. How could the world be so beautiful and so cruel at the same time?

"Bhag Bhari, are you feeling well?" asked Jeeti with a concerned expression. "I sincerely hope you've stopped all this warrior practice with Gurdas."

"Pitaji caught us, and he forbade me to see Gurdas again. Pitaji isn't speaking to me now." I avoided looking at Jeeti.

"You knew this would happen. I don't blame your father. Somebody needed to be firm with you. Playing with swords is no way for a woman to behave." Jeeti turned away from me to play with a blade of grass. Then she turned to face me again; this time, her voice was soft and low. "I know how close you are to your cousin. It must be hard to no longer be allowed to see him."

"There's more." I spoke quickly. "Gurdas and my mamaji are leaving to fight alongside our Guru in four nights' time. And I cannot do anything about it." My knee began to tremble.

Jeeti's jaw dropped, and she leaned forward to hug me. Her comforting embrace grounded me. She looked solemn, seeming unsure of how to respond. But I was glad to have her with me.

Perhaps, there wasn't anything to say.

The morning of their departure, I busied myself with chores, desperate for a distraction. I went looking for Dilbagh to help me carry some wood, stopping short when I spotted him in a quiet conversation with Gurdas.

"I may not see you again, Veer. I fulfill my dharam with pride, but if anything happens to my pitaji and me, please take care of my mother and sister. Vaada karo," whispered Gurdas.

Dilbagh hugged him tight, and Gurdas's body racked with great big sobs, his chest rising and falling with short, abrupt breaths. I cupped my hands over my mouth to conceal my yelp of surprise. I wanted to run and comfort him, but I couldn't.

He was supposed to be my strong, older cousin who protected and comforted me, not the other way around. I wasn't going to snatch that respect away from him.

Our families assembled in front of our house to bid Mamaji and Gurdas farewell. They tied baskets to their horses and loaded them with a few personal belongings and provisions. I could see dark circles under their eyes—they hadn't slept well. Each wore a mighty kirpan at his hip. I spotted a few daggers and other weapons hidden in their clothing. My cousin carried a toradar slung across his torso. He looked so young and small, diminished by the fierce-looking matchlock musket.

I made eye contact with Mamaji as he mounted his horse, and he smiled. A rush of emotions passed through me—joy and sadness, honor and dharam, service and sacrifice. *But isn't that what life is? Then why am I crying?*

My mamaji gestured for me to come toward him. "You are my beloved Bhag Bhari and always will be. The sole recipient of the sweetest mangoes I can pluck." He stroked my hair gently. Would that be the last time I would feel his loving touch? Gurdas, on the other hand, didn't meet anyone's gaze. My dear, loving cousin was clearly torn up inside, and I couldn't do a thing. *I need to go with him.*

"Fight with honor! You will live on for eternity! Death before tyranny!" my pitaji shouted as they rode off.

I could hardly swallow—the lump in my throat had grown so large. Mataji was clutching the end of her red chunni and twisting it in her clasped hands. Mamiji was crying uncontrollably. My mother spoke to her quietly and led her into our home.

Returning outside after a while, Mataji smoothed out her salwar-kameez and pulled her chunni over her head. "Before we start our chores, why don't I tell you a story about one of our Gurus? Let's eat breakfast together."

As children, my veere and I would sit in front of our mother and listen in wonder to the stories she told us about the divine Gurus. Sometimes she surprised us with new stories, pretending to pull them out from a secret compartment of her mind where she had stored them for safekeeping. I had tucked each story away like a precious gem, never knowing when I might need them in life.

This time, though, Mataji's storytelling felt different. I was old enough to understand she wanted to distract us from the morning's event, especially my young cousin Jasmeet. The war no longer seemed like a far-off thing, something that affected strangers. Not anymore. My family, like a thread woven into fabric, was now intricately linked to history.

We sat on jute mats under the shade of our peepul tree, its branches heavy with bitter, grapelike fruit. Bees hovered over a patch of flowers nearby, their wings iridescent in the sunlight.

Mataji prepared a tray of fruits, pickles, and yogurt to accompany the steaming hot, ghee-soaked parate straight from the chulha. We scrambled to grab a buttery flatbread each as soon as she set the plate down. Mataji spoke, as she always did, by telling us the ways in which each Guru gifted us.

"Our first Guru gave humankind salvation."

There were too many stories about our first Guru to count. I used to imagine I was there with him, listening to his beautiful poetry about Waheguru. The thought would send shivers down my spine.

My mother's voice brought me back to the present. "With this story, I will share my understanding of what happened as it was passed down from my parents to me and from their parents before them. By sharing these stories, we keep our faith alive. Our Guru's following is young, but we cannot let oppression extinguish our beliefs. I will teach you, as you must teach your bachche."

"Is that why Veerji and Pitaji went to battle? To fight this oppression?" Jasmeet piped up, scooping up cool yogurt with a piece of parata. Her chubby little fingers were covered in melted ghee. Jasmeet's baby curls framed her innocent face, and my heart ached for what she understood about her family's fate. I swallowed the last of my parata and wrapped my arms around her, careful not to interrupt her eating.

"Ha, Dhi." Mataji's eyelids dropped. "The first Guru and his companion, Mardana, traveled to a distant village. They were not welcome there, and the inhabitants were mean and stingy, set on finding fault with each other." Mataji flicked away a pesky mosquito and continued, "There are people who will not be there for you, no matter what you do, bachche." Mataji looked at me, and for a moment, I believed she might understand me more than I thought.

We nodded, except for Jasmeet, who wiped a streak of yogurt from her cheek.

"The Guru told the villagers they should continue to live together as a community. They then moved on to a neighboring village. The people there were kind and generous, and the Guru told the villagers they should disperse to the four corners of the earth. His friend Mardana was confused."

Chotu wrinkled his brow. "You mean the unkind people should stay together and kind people should not?"

"Yes, that is what Mardana asked." Mataji raised her eyebrows to indicate she was getting to the answer. "Guru Nanak Dev Ji explained that the first group would only spread their sullenness to people elsewhere, but the second set would share good values by their gentle example." Mataji smiled.

"I still don't understand why good people should separate," said Chotu as he nestled into Mataji's lap. She wrapped her arms around him.

I understood the Guru's wisdom. There were people who found fault with the way I walked, the way I talked, the way I behaved. I thought of Kulwinder and the village kuriyaan who teased me. It felt like someone was waiting to disapprove of me at every turn. Dilbagh did it almost every day. Sometimes it felt as if blinking my eyes would be cause for judgment. I have learned to stay away from those who want to find fault with me, who try to extinguish the fire within me. I am afraid if I allow them to do it long enough, they just might succeed.

We finished our breakfast, and Mataji paused her storytelling. "We need to tend to our chores now."

My veere retrieved axes from the side of the house. I drew water from the well for Mataji and me to cook lunch. Jasmeet was at my heels all day. It irked me to see my brothers chop wood, till the fields, and care for our horses. I'd rather do those things than cook and clean. I paused to give my cousin a turn at sweeping the floors and glared at my veere. *Gadhe.*

"Bhag Bhari, stop dawdling. We need milk." Mataji paid no notice to my growing irritation. I huffed and puffed as we set off to milk the cows. Fresh milk meant we could make curd that evening and enjoy white butter and ghee the following day. Annoyed as I was, I couldn't help feeling a bit hungry at the thought.

After milking the cows, I returned to find Chotu sprawled out beneath the shade of the peepul tree. I poked him with a stick and reminded him that our second Guru worked an honest job making manji. "You are a disappointment, Chotu." I jumped on top of him, and we tickled each other until we were helpless with laughter.

"Till the death!" Chotu tackled me as he squeezed his hands into my armpits. I guffawed and reached for his feet to tickle his heels.

"Stop! Stop!" His laughter sprinkled the air like spices on subji. Jasmeet giggled and covered her mouth with her hand.

Just then, my mamiji emerged from inside, her eyes puffy and red. "Jasmeet Dhi, enough. It's time to go home now."

# FIVE

E arly the following day, my mother poked me until I opened my eyes. "Wake up. We have to make ghee."

The sky was clear except for the faint outline of the moon and a few scattered stars. Darkness blanketed the earth, save for the fireflies that appeared and disappeared, flickering like starlight. We had to rise before the sun so the curds Mataji prepared the night before would still be cool in their clay pots. Cool curds made solid butter, which was easier to skim off the top of buttermilk than a creamier butter. I was not sure when I'd learned this fact, but it felt as though I'd known it since birth.

Mataji placed the large clay pot of curds in front of one of the pillars on our porch. She wrapped a long rope around the column and looped it around a butter churn and back. She then handed me the loose ends, and I had to pull the rope back and forth to rotate the churn. Tedious work, like most of my chores.

After a while, my arms went limp. "I can't do anymore. My shoulders are exhausted!"

Mataji stood up. "Dhi, you should have said something. If you are tired, sit down and rest." She picked up the stick and churned at twice the speed I had managed. Mataji never complained—if her arms ached, she didn't show it. What was wrong with me? If I couldn't even churn butter, I had no right to train as a warrior. Fighting required tremendous endurance, and here I was, whining about my shoulders. Mataji was more fit for battle than me.

The air soon filled with the staccato music of golden orioles. The sun rose, staining the sky with pinks and oranges and yellows as it warmed up our land. I sat on the porch, sucking on a ripe mango from our harvest, sticky juice running down my hands. I remembered that Mamaji would save the sweetest mangoes he could find for me, and I missed him.

"Mataji, will Hindustan ever be peaceful?" I asked.

Mataji stopped mid-churn. "More peaceful than this? We have good food and our family is together. Dhi, you are worrying yourself with matters that don't concern you."

"Don't concern me because I'm a kuri?" I wiped stray bits of mango from my cheeks.

"No, because you are too young, and you are my bachcha. So, I must protect you," replied Mataji, in an attempt to end my interrogation.

"What if Gurdas and Mamaji die?" I couldn't stop myself; my tongue formed words of its own will.

"Then Waheguru will give them salvation," Mataji snapped at me, but her eyes looked sad. She hit the churn with more force than necessary to shake off the bits of butter stuck to the rod. "It's done. Let's separate the lassi from the butter." From her tone, Mataji meant our conversation was over. I had been unsympathetic to her feelings, and I regretted my cruel words.

We scraped the butter from the top of the pot and transferred it to another clay vessel, which we placed on the chulha. Unable to resist the temptation any longer, I grabbed the pot with the lassi and lifted it to my mouth. The sweet, creamy liquid drizzled down my throat. Mataji watched me with an amused expression before taking a sip of her own.

Soon, everyone was up. We feasted on buttery parate for breakfast that morning. Pitaji sat next to me. "Dhi, the butter you and your mataji made is delicious."

Now that Gurdas and Mamaji had left our village, he was talking to me again. *Convenient.* We ate quietly because no one had the nerve to voice their innermost worries. We were trained to scrub them from our minds, like sweeping dust off the floors.

"Gurdas loves fresh butter." My words rang out in the silence. I couldn't help myself; it was only human to miss him.

"Gurdas and your mamaji are following their dharam, just as you are when you make butter for your family," growled Pitaji, his eyes threatening me to stop. Dilbagh glared at me. *Death before tyranny. I won't be silenced.*

My eyes welled with tears, and Pitaji reached for my hand, but the damage was done.

"I'm not hungry." I jumped up and ran toward the fields, seeking a secluded area.

I stretched out on the dirt, hidden by the long stalks of grass. *I can determine my own dharam.* Our third Guru preached that everyone was created equal. If he were still alive, I could be a soldier in the Khalsa army. My wrestling skills and my aim would be assets on the battlefield. The thought of being on the front alongside the Guru was no longer a passing daydream. I could feel it in my bones.

I picked up a long stick and jumped up to practice my sword strikes. "Ja!" I said, challenging an imaginary opponent.

My thoughts wandered as I practiced. Being a warrior was my heritage, passed down from my pitaji, who received it from his father. Memories of my dadaji sparring with my great-uncle Langah drifted my way. Momentarily blinded by the sun, I paused to catch my breath and cover my eyes with my forearm.

The sun was bright, just like the day we visited Sri Harmandir Sahib Gurdwara in Amritsar. I could still feel that frisson of excitement when we entered the sanctum and heard our Holy Book, the Adi Granth, being recited. The fifth Guru had spent many seasons compiling sacred compositions into one tome. The Guru's painstaking effort was a reminder that the work we do in our lives has the power to transcend us and leave an imprint on the hearts and minds of generations to come. I dropped my stick and stared at my hands, wondering if they held that sort of grace.

I couldn't be sure how long I'd disappeared before I heard Mataji call, "Dhi, where are you? I need your help."

Mataji handed me a dish brimming with atta, wheat flour, and a jug of water. We squatted side by side, and I began kneading the dough while my mother peeled an onion.

Mataji spoke softly, "With Mamaji and your cousin away, your father and I will be responsible for managing both families. There is no time to play in the fields. Do you understand, Dhi?"

"Yes." I worked the dough. "I am worried about Veer and Mamaji. No one in our family talks about it."

Mataji softened, and she opened her mouth to respond, but my aunt and Jasmeet appeared. Chotu rounded the corner toward us, as well. My veer scooped Jasmeet up and threw her in the air, catching her under her armpits as she fell. He spun her around in circles until they fell on the floor, dizzy and disoriented. Mataji wordlessly rolled out rotis.

It was a tough time for all of us—especially Mamiji. She sat down on a manji. "Satwant of our village lost her husband. You know who she is, right? She has three young children. I spent all day there yesterday, helping her with her chores. She is so proud of him, but she is also in distress. Emperor Aurangzeb's soldiers number in the thousands. We don't have enough men to fight back."

"Maybe we should train?" I shocked myself with the audacity of my words.

Mataji looked up in alarm, and the roti she was flipping on the chulha almost slipped from her hand. She caught it just before the flames consumed it.

Mamiji slapped my thigh and laughed. "So many women

are caring for homes and farms and children alone. If we can manage all of this by ourselves, can't we manage a little skirmish?"

My mataji raised her hand as if to smack me, and her lips thinned. *When will she stop lying to herself about me?* Pitaji had caught me training with Gurdas, and Mataji knew I wrestled with boys in the village.

Mamiji looked away, oblivious to the tension in the air. She got up and walked away toward the fields.

Pitaji and Dilbagh joined us. "What is happening here?" Pitaji eyed us, straight-faced.

"Bhag Bhari thinks because women till the fields, they can also stand up to the Mughals." Mataji spoke with a quiet fury. She crossed her arms.

"Nonsense." Pitaji took a couple of steps toward me, his eyes wide. I straightened my back and furrowed my brow.

"Bhen, the battlefield is no place for you," said Dilbagh, turning his head away from me.

"I am the most skilled warrior in this family after Pitaji." I glared at my brother.

Dilbagh scowled, wincing at my jab, then got up and walked away without uttering another word. *Oy! How convenient for him to tell me how to live my life and never have to think twice about his behavior.*

"We must understand our dharam, our place in life. Yours is to take care of the home, like Jeeti and me. You should not scoff at the importance of this. You need to think about marriage and starting a family. This is how we survive as a community," said Mataji. She paused and looked at me; her mouth opened and closed before allowing the words to come out. "We are seeking a suitable match for you."

The shock rendered me immobile. *Marriage?* I knew this day would come, but to have it thrust upon me like this was jarring. I wanted to respect my family's wishes, but this went against my hopes and desires. I bit my bottom lip, holding back tears. Jeeti had gushed about marriage, but in all that time, she had never really listened to me. It was lonely being different. I missed my cousin Gurdas.

"I will never stop wanting to fight. That is what I was created for. Our people are at risk of being annihilated, and every day, more men die fighting. And I will never want to marry if I cannot take up arms to protect us." I felt unsure of myself, but I held my head high and feigned conviction. "If Mamaji and Gurdas die, then we all deserve the pain we will feel, since we did not fight with honor alongside them." I stood up to walk away.

Mataji stood up and seized my wrist. "Get this out of your head. You are our dhi, and you will marry and raise a family."

"Let go of my hand, Mataji. You're hurting me!" I yanked my hand from her grip with a jerk. My mother stumbled backward. Pitaji stared at me with bloodshot eyes, but he didn't say a word. He turned his back on me and walked away.

I understood what my family expected from me, and I knew they believed what they were doing for me was for the best. But standing back and doing nothing when people were dying—that was not dharam. Not mine, at least.

# SIX

Winter passed with no word from my uncle and cousin. Our village received periodic news of men who had died in battle. Each time, I held my breath and begged Waheguru to protect my mamaji and cousin. *Are they cold? Are they hungry? Are they alive?* We prayed regularly for the health of our tenth Guru and our people.

My family rose early one cool morning to the gentle chirping of birds. I stretched and tilted my face upward to look at the puffy white clouds. The sun's rays warmed my skin like divine kisses, and I savored this tiny moment of happiness.

I drew a pail of water from the well and was stuffing some dirty clothes into the bucket, when all of a sudden, I was soaking wet.

"Ahhh!" Ice-cold water dripped down the side of my face, and a puddle formed around my feet.

"Got you!" exclaimed Chotu, laughing as he ran away. He wasn't fast enough—I caught up to him and landed a handful of mud right in his smug face.

"Bhenji, you are disgusting!" said Chotu, trying to wipe the muddy residue off his cheeks with his free hand.

"You deserved it. You harassed me first."

Just then, Mataji called us in to eat. She looked at Chotu and me, dripping wet and streaked with mud, and lowered her eyes in disinterest.

Mamiji dropped Jasmeet off, saying, "I need to clean the house and cook. Jasmeet will be underfoot, and the work will take twice as long." Gurdas wasn't there to play with Jasmeet. "Behave yourself, Dhi." She hugged my cousin and left.

My veere, cousin, and I sat on jute mats beneath the shaded peepul tree and ate generous helpings of ghee-soaked parate, so warm and flaky that they crumbled at our touch. I used a piece of flatbread to scoop up cool homemade yogurt and then smeared a dash of mango pickle to create the perfect bite. My veere inhaled their food, with not so much as a pause between bites.

"Hmph, behaving as though you haven't eaten in ages. No one helped me make this tasty food either. Besharam." *Shameless.*

We finished eating, and a pair of jackdaws landed on the tree branch above our heads. Chotu jumped up and shook the tree, and the birds skittered in a flurry.

Mataji scooped up two pots. "Time for chores now. Come, Bhag Bhari, help me."

I didn't follow her right away. I chose instead to lie under the tree with my siblings. My veere and I did not always get along, but my heart swelled with love for them. Dilbagh's dour nature balanced Chotu's silliness. These brief moments with them shone like the brightest stars at night.

One of us spotted Pitaji's bow and arrows leaning against a wall. He had forgotten to put them away. Dilbagh and I raced to get them, but he grabbed them just before me. He then positioned himself in front of a target etched in a tree and took aim. He missed by half an arm's length.

I snagged the bow from him and retrieved an arrow from the quiver. I placed my left foot in front of my right and positioned the arrow in perfect alignment with the target before releasing it. Dead-on. I didn't stop there. Four arrows, one after the other, hit the mark on the tree. There was a certain cadence to archery, almost like a dance—the act of drawing the arrow, nocking it, and then letting it fly.

"Look, my veer! Did you learn something today?"

"You don't need to shoot arrows, Bhenji. That is a man's job," said Dilbagh. His snide comment lit a fire in me, and I charged at him but stopped in my tracks when I noticed Pitaji watching us. Dilbagh looked like he'd been punched in the stomach—he wasn't supposed to touch our father's weapons without his permission. We stood there, frozen.

"Bhag Bhari, your aim was perfect. You were right. Chotu and Dilbagh need lessons from you on marksmanship. But what if your aim was slightly off, and one of the arrows struck Chotu? Don't ever touch my weapons again."

Pitaji looked at my brothers. "I will work with Chotu and Dilbagh on their skills. Put the bow and arrows back where you found them." He turned to walk away.

"You will work with Dilbagh and Chotu, though I am more skilled than them?" I yelled, my cursed tongue unable to control itself.

Pitaji moved toward me and waved his finger in my face. "Did you just speak back to me? I am your father."

"Yes, show some respect, Bhenji." Dilbagh's pompous expression made my blood boil.

"Shut your mouth, Dilbagh. I may train you, but you also shot an arrow without my permission," chided Pitaji, glowering at my veer.

"Pitaji, I respect you, but you did not answer me. Why will you only work with Chotu and Dilbagh if I am the better marksman?"

"You must understand your dharam," said Pitaji, looking at me pensively.

"I do understand, but maybe my dharam is twofold." I let my words hang in the air.

"Perhaps. But the three of you will not touch my weapons again. Those weapons are meant to kill, and you will injure yourselves unless you've been properly trained." He walked away.

I stormed into the house, Jasmeet at my heels, and found Mataji munching on a radish. "Come to help me?" asked Mataji, looking exasperated. She was oblivious to my feelings. "I need water."

Jasmeet and I set off to fetch water from the well, when I heard quick, heavy footsteps nearing us. Mataji, who heard them as well, rushed out of the home. We turned in the direction of the sound.

It was my aunt running toward us at full tilt.

My mamiji's hair was a mess; her jumbled bun splayed on top of her head. She wore mismatched clothes. Her eyes were puffy and red. Mamiji collapsed on the ground in front of my mother and wrapped her arms around Mataji's legs. She rested her wet cheek against Mataji's thigh. Jasmeet ran toward her mother, her long braids slapping her back.

*No. Not that. It can't be . . .*

"They are gone!" she sobbed. "My husband—your veer—and my puttar are dead! We will never see them again in this lifetime."

My mother sank to the ground. I ran to her and wrapped my arms around her body. It felt like she had shrunk in the time it took me to reach her. Her eyes glazed over, but she had no tears.

Chotu hugged my cousin. Dilbagh yelled, looking for Pitaji. His cry rang out in the fields, and Pitaji came running toward us. He surveyed the scene and immediately knew.

Mamiji spoke again through her sobs, "They died more than fifteen nights ago."

Their bodies were brought to Jhabal Kalan by another warrior, wrapped in muslin shrouds, and placed beyond our fields so that we could give them an honorable farewell. Gurdas was barely older than me, and now he was gone.

"I will die with them! I am already dead!" Mamiji shouted

through tears. My mother cupped her hand over Mamiji's mouth to silence her. Pitaji walked over to Mataji and placed his hand on her shoulder. His face looked solemn, and we understood that this was his way of showing devotion. *Death before tyranny.* I noticed the lines stretching across his forehead for the first time. Crow's feet extended from his tired eyes. When had he aged so much?

He walked away and retrieved an axe from the side of the hut. He left to chop wood, to give Mamaji and Gurdas a respectable cremation. We moved through a haze. Our elders prepared the bodies for the last rites; we weren't allowed to go with them. I needed time alone, so I sneaked out with Pitaji's sword to the woods.

The sounds of chirping cicadas filled my ears. Deeper in the greenery, a herd of deer trotted through the lush foliage. I finally found even ground next to a kikar tree, its spherical yellow flowers spreading out like a delicate carpet under my feet. I'd never borrowed Pitaji's kirpan, but playing with sticks no longer challenged me.

I unsheathed the sword and sliced at a tree trunk, imagining the tree to be the soldiers who ended my mamaji's and cousin's lives. I swung and swung until my body was ready to collapse.

We didn't cook dinner that evening, satisfying our grumbling bellies with fruit and raw vegetables. When Pitaji came home, I watched him walk to our neighbor Jaswant Uncle's house.

I was behind our house collecting wood and decided to follow him in secret. Jaswant Uncle had received the bodies and had spoken to the warrior who brought them to our village. I hid behind a tree to listen in on their conversation.

"Sat Sri Akal Ji," said Pitaji. Their eyes met before they stared at their feet. Respect for the dead, I supposed. "Do you know how my brother-in-law and nephew died?"

Jaswant Uncle, clearly uncomfortable to be the bearer of bad news, spoke softly, his eyes still downcast. "Veerji, they fought without fear and died with their heads held high. The warrior told me that a sword struck your nephew in his heart, and he died instantly. He did not suffer."

In war, you took what you could get. A lack of suffering was considered good luck. But Gurdas was dead! How could his death be considered lucky? My blood boiled. I shoved my fist into my mouth to stop from screaming.

Jaswant Uncle looked as though he was praying for my father to walk away. Pitaji nodded in understanding and said, "I have seen the bodies. You don't need to hide anything from me. I just want to know if my brother-in-law suffered."

Mamaji was like a second father to me and considered me his dhi. He would save the sweetest mangoes for me. He even let me look at his weapons, aware of my fascination. I should have walked away at that moment, but something kept me rooted to the spot.

Jaswant Uncle's eyes filled with tears. "Your brother-in-law was one of the finest men I knew. Your family has been honored by his sacrifice to his dharam and his Guru."

"I am immensely proud of him. But please, I need to know," said Pitaji, his head lowered in respect.

"Your brother-in-law faced an immoral and heartless opponent. He dismembered him and left him to bleed to death." He looked up at my pitaji and said, "Your brother-in-law suffered terribly in death, but his honorable actions will secure him the highest place with Waheguru."

That was the last thing I heard. And then everything went black.

When I awoke, I was on the ground with my head on Mataji's lap. We were seated near the well in front of our hut, and my face was wet. Someone had tried to wake me.

"Mein sadke jawan. Bhag Bhari is awake. Are you in pain, Dhi?" Mataji asked, her voice anxious.

"My head hurts, but I am well. Don't worry." I tried to stand up, but my head felt like someone was attacking it with a brick. Dizzy and nauseated, I lay back down. I could make out the forms of my pitaji and my veere standing over me. Chotu's eyes were red and his face puffy.

"Your pitaji heard a heavy thud and found you lying behind a tree. You hit your head, Dhi. What made you think listening in on your elders was a good idea?" Mataji asked.

"They were my family, too. I had to know. And you will not tell me anything."

"I hope this puts all the absurd ideas of fighting out of your head. You can't even hear about such things without fainting," declared Mataji, waving her hand dismissively.

I did not sleep that night. Alone under the stars, I cried my heart out. I let my tears flood my body and fill my soul.

I closed my eyes and saw my mamaji's eyes light up like they used to whenever he saw me. I heard his big belly laugh. His hands were often dirty and calloused—the hands of a man who worked hard all his life. He used them to till the soil, chop wood, and wield his sword. He used those hands to hug his children and stroke their hair.

I remembered feeling my cousin's fear before he set off. He didn't meet anyone's eyes that morning, afraid he might break down, and now he was gone forever. They sacrificed their lives for a cause we knew to be just. My mind told me this, but my heart refused to accept their loss.

In the morning, their bodies were placed atop a pile of wood just beyond our fields. My pitaji lit the pyre. Chotu stood there shaking at the sight of flames shooting up toward the sky. Mamiji fell to the ground and wrapped her arms around herself. Her guttural cries were the only sound in the crisp morning air.

I learned that my relatives died trying to defend the kingdom of Guler. When the Raja of Guler failed to pay a hefty tribute to the Mughal throne, Aurangzeb's soldiers pounced on the kingdom. Seven Sikhs, emissaries of peace sent by Guru Gobind Singh Ji, perished in the attack. The Raja of Guler was victorious that day, but a family in Jhabal Kalan had lost two precious souls.

Later that afternoon, my mother was nowhere to be found. I looked everywhere—our home, our fields, even our neighbors' homes—before heading to the cremation grounds. There she was, squatting on the ground, her hands covering her face. I sank to the ground as quietly as I could, fearful she might ask me to leave.

She didn't. Instead, she spoke in a quiet voice, "I'm struggling to remember the sound of my veerji's voice, the jokes and stories he would tell us." Mataji took a deep breath. "And . . . Gurdas loved my saag on a cold winter day. How can I make it now without feeding him?" She shivered, her eyes blank and unseeing. I listened in silence and squeezed her hand gently.

She continued, "They say Waheguru teaches us lessons to bring us closer to Him, but in these moments of pain, I feel so alone. Then, all at once, a feeling washes over me, as though some healing force is filling me up. I breathe and close my eyes and hope to hold on to this feeling for as long as I can before the pain takes over again." Mataji stopped and dabbed her eyes with her chunni. "I tell myself this is Waheguru, although I am not certain. These waves come and go. They don't get better with time; rather, you become accustomed to them and hope to focus on the good." She rested her head on my shoulder, and I wrapped my arms around her. It was strange, because this is how she held me when I was a child. Until today, I had never seen her cry.

Time went on, as it does, and one day Mataji awoke more cheerful than she had been since my cousin and mamaji died. We spent the day together. We laughed and told stories as we worked—for the first time in what felt like forever.

That night, my brothers and I were lounging under a tree when our mother walked over to us. She spoke to us as if she were telling us one of her instructive tales about the Gurus. "Your cousin and mamaji died with the highest honor. We will remember them as strong and fearless men who fought against injustice. In telling their story, we will find the light to guide us through the darkness."

# SEVEN

It was my sixteenth spring, and wildflowers' chaotic stems twisted in the joy of new life, flashing petals brighter than a deeva, a lamp. The sun bloomed on the horizon, filling the sky with shades of orange and pink and stretching outward into the ever-present blue. It radiated hope, a new beginning. Another chance at life.

It was almost time for the festival of Baisakhi, and Guru Gobind Singh Ji had called all his followers to Anandpur Sahib, the City of Bliss. Several seasons had come and gone since the passing of my cousin and uncle. Since their tragic deaths, we hadn't left our village. This was the first trip we were embarking on as a family.

On the second day of our pilgrimage, we stopped near Kapurthala to rest under the shade of a jamun tree. My brothers and I climbed the branches to gather handfuls of the tart purple berries. I chewed on the oblong fruit, sucking in my cheeks with each sour bite. Jamun were sweet in the summertime, but they had few takers in spring. My pitaji stuffed handfuls of fruit into his mouth. As he chewed, the tiny berries burst, and juice dripped down his thick, graying beard. He laughed and wiped his mouth with his free hand. I loved how his eyes smiled when his mouth did, like faithful friends.

Mataji rested in the shade. She covered her sun-dappled face with her mango-yellow chunni to block out the light filtering through the tree's canopy. Only a few strands of dark hair held out in a crown of silver atop her head.

"Eat the rotis I made. We have a long journey ahead, and you will need sustenance," she said, peeking from behind her chunni.

My brothers had grown into strong men, built like my pitaji. They were taller than me now and seemed to grow more with every sunrise. Chotu was lean and muscled, and his speed made him nimble with a sword. Dilbagh was well-built and powerful—a formidable wrestler. Dark hairs sprouted from their sun-browned faces, and their hands had hardened and calloused with labor.

Dilbagh unsheathed his sword and vigorously polished it with a cloth, while Chotu knelt and placed a bucket full of water in front of Sher. Our thirsty horse lowered his muzzle and slurped as he drank, his throat pulsating as he swallowed.

I had grown into a woman, my body filling out more than I liked. Mataji had noticed and remarked, "Be thankful for those wide hips. Childbirth will be easy for you."

I sat with my eyes closed, leaning against the trunk of the jamun tree, and imagined meeting the Guru for the first time.

"Wake up, Bhenji." Dilbagh shook me awake. "We still have quite a distance to cover. This is no time to fall asleep."

"Let her sleep. We will be traveling on foot for a long time, and all of us require rest," said my pitaji as he waved him away. "In any event, it is not advisable to travel at midday because of the heat."

My family arrived in Anandpur Sahib after journeying for seven nights. The soles of my feet were covered with calluses, and my legs throbbed in pain. We arrived ragged and empty-bellied. But as we entered the city, we sensed a palpable excitement in the air. I felt renewed, like taking a dip in a river on a sweltering day. I was going to meet our Guru, messenger of Waheguru, and be anointed a true Sikh. What greater blessing could there be for a loyal follower?

We climbed uphill to the tent where the community, the sangat, had gathered. The cacophony hit us like a brick—laughter and gossip, swords clanging in play, and the raucous shouts of a warrior community gathered in one place. It smelled of sweat and cooking fires. But food must wait.

A large tent had been erected to provide shade in the sweltering heat. We squeezed through the crowds to find an opening, and when we did, we sat down quickly. In front of us, our Guru sat on a throne, dressed in white. An ornate turban adorned with a large gemstone and topped with a white plume crowned his head. A dark beard highlighted his sharp jawline. His weapons drew the eye to his broad-shouldered, muscular body. A beautiful white hawk, one of the birds of prey he was famous for rearing, perched on his forearm. His skills as a falconer earned the Guru the nickname Chittian Bazaan Wale. His face shone bright with divine light; he seemed to possess an almost otherworldly grace.

Once the sangat had settled, the Guru stood up and drew his sword. His powerful stance commanded the attention of the crowd.

"Our fellow Sikhs are dying every day on the battlefield, murdered in unimaginable ways. It causes me immense pain to tell you that I have cremated countless bodies. These were loyal fathers and brothers, beloved sons and husbands. We are being slaughtered for our beliefs, for our refusal to pay an unjust tax to keep a cruel emperor in power. We will never submit to tyranny. We are the Pure. We are the Khalsa." He exuded power in waves so strong they knocked the sangat back in our seats.

The cheer that went up was deafening. The Guru paused for a moment, and his eyes approvingly roved over the crowd. "My veere and bhene, remember that the enemy is not religion. The enemy is the oppressor who misuses religion. The temple and the mosque are the same. They lead to the same end. We must recognize the human race as one." The sangat, now entranced, hung on to the Guru's every utterance as though it were divine nectar. "And yet, in order to safeguard our rights, warriors should fulfill their dharam and fight for justice. Love for a neighbor must accompany the punishment of a trespasser. Service of saints requires the annihilation of tyrants. For this reason, I bow with devotion to the holy sword."

He lowered his head for a moment and then spoke again. "Every great deed is preceded by sacrifice. Is there a devoted

Sikh who will give his head to me here and now?" the Guru demanded.

A hush fell over the assembly; the faces around me looked horror-stricken. *What did I just hear?* A shockwave coursed through me in slow motion, as if my body was unable to process the Guru's words. Chotu grabbed my hand, and I clasped his clammy fingers. The Guru then repeated his request, this time in a sterner tone.

After the third time, a man stood up. "I am Daya Ram of Lahore. I am ready to sacrifice myself for you, dear Guru, and the Khalsa. Without our devotion, we are nothing!" With these words, Daya Ram followed the Guru, who led him into another tent.

A few tense moments later, the Guru returned alone, his sword stained with blood, and demanded another head. The crowd gasped in terror. Chotu was trembling in fear, and I could barely breathe. Did our Guru kill Daya Ram? I couldn't believe that our revered Guru was capable of such cold violence. I had only seen love in his warm eyes.

Before I could gather my thoughts, another man stood up. "I am Dharam Das, and I sacrifice my very soul to you." The crowd parted to allow him to walk up to the front. As before, the Guru returned alone with a bloody sword. On his face was an expression of peace, not murderous rage—something didn't feel right. The pieces didn't fit together.

The hairs on my neck stood up. I willed myself to understand, but it felt like an impossible task. People in the crowd wailed. A wild-eyed woman in a green salwar-kameez sobbed uncontrollably, pounding the ground where Dharam Das sat not a few minutes ago. His wife? Or his bhen? The people around her tried to console her, grasping at her flailing arms. But how did you contain an ocean of grief?

The Guru's voice rang out, "Who else will sacrifice themselves for the Khalsa?"

I prayed fervently that no one from my family would volunteer. A group of men in identical peacock-blue turbans rose abruptly and stormed out of the tent. Next to Mataji, a guava-faced woman perspired like a warrior in battle. Behind us, a silver-bearded man closed his eyes and sang to himself.

Mohkam Chand stood as the next volunteer. "I am at your command, Guru Ji, and I sacrifice myself to you!" A young kuri, presumably his daughter, wrapped her arms around his leg, and he dragged her with him until her arms gave way. She screamed when he disappeared into the second tent, an excruciating sound that pierced our ears. I shifted closer to my mataji, and she wrapped her arms around me, her face emotionless. I looked at my pitaji; his face betrayed no fear. I could almost hear his thoughts—*Death before tyranny!*

Himmat Rai and Sahib Chand were the fourth and fifth men to stand up. The pungent odor of sweaty bodies in the tent surrounded us like a thick fog. My stomach roiled, and I swallowed the bile rising to my mouth. How could this be helping our cause? How could murdering our own people save us?

"Bhen, do not worry. We must trust in the Guru," said Dilbagh gently.

My brother's fear had morphed into something else—belief? Was this what true faith looked like?

"The next time he asks for a head, you'd better not volunteer," I whispered in his ear. *Should I volunteer instead? Would he accept a woman's sacrifice?*

Each time the Guru returned, he remained calm, his face exuding benevolence. The guava-faced aunty held her knees as she rocked back and forth. She recited a prayer, her tears mixed with sweat pouring down her cheeks. Members of the sangat cried and screamed, while others shook their heads in disbelief. Many stormed out of the tent. A rope-thin older woman in a far corner of the tent doubled over, retching. A young boy rubbed her back and held her sweaty hair away from her face. Perhaps she was a family member of one of the newly deceased?

This time, the Guru didn't reappear. Bolder voices within the sangat demanded answers. *Why were these senseless killings necessary?* Others countered with their faith. *He is our Guru, and who are we to question our savior? He will give us answers in time.*

And then, much to my surprise, Dilbagh stood up and yelled, "We bow to our Guru's wisdom. Death before tyranny!" The crowd cheered.

Outside, ominous-looking gray-black clouds closed in around the tent, when suddenly, the sun's rays broke through and shone upon us. Right then, the Guru emerged from the tent with the five volunteers, all of them hale and hearty. They were dressed in fine silk robes and saffron-colored turbans. Each had a garland of flowers around his neck. The five men stood tall and proud. Our Guru had not harmed them!

The sangat went wild in relief, and suddenly it felt like we were at a wedding instead of a funeral. Mataji quietly sighed, and the color returned to Chotu's face. My pitaji nodded in respect.

"The great Guru is merciful," a devotee in the crowd shouted. "He lifts us up!" cheered another.

A young boy spun in joyful circles. Mokham Chand's daughter sprinted to her pitaji and threw her arms around him. The Guru's actions had terrified me, but now I felt proud. The men who volunteered had overcome the most debilitating enemy of all—fear. For a faithful warrior, death was not the end, but the beginning of eternal life. The sangat settled down, and the joyful chaos subsided. All eyes were trained on the Guru.

The Guru raised his hand to silence us. "You are my brothers and sisters. Those of you who take this blessed nectar, this amrit, become my lions and lionesses, my Singhs and Kaurs. My beloved five, the panj pyare, will now be known as Daya Singh, Dharam Singh, Mohkam Singh, Himmat Singh, and Sahib Singh."

We roared our approval. I was now Bhag Kaur, and my veere and pitaji took the name Singh. The common titles meant there was no difference between members of our community.

The Guru stood with his feet hip-distance apart and raised both hands. "My Sikhs, you must carry the panj kakaar, the five symbols of your faith, upon your person: unshorn hair, or kes; a kanga, or comb; a sword, the kirpan; a garment for modesty, or kashera; and a metal bracelet, or kara. You must live according to Guru Nanak Dev Ji's rules for life: Naam, Daan, and Ishaan. Meditate on Waheguru's name, share the fruit of your earnings with the needy, and purify yourself daily."

I memorized his words, holding on to them like a warrior grips their sword. *This is how I will honor my Guru and myself.*

Our Guru then clasped his double-edged sword, the khanda. The ornate broadsword looked heavy, but he made it seem as light as my wooden practice weapon. He picked up a large bowl of sugar-sweetened water and stirred it with the khanda, reciting prayer hymns.

One by one, the panj pyare knelt before the Guru and drank from the bowl, each taking a sip of the blessed amrit. Guru Gobind Singh Ji then sprinkled the nectar over their heads. Finally, each man offered the Guru a sip of nectar at his request.

From the crowd came a shout. "Guru Ji, bravo! You are divine and a true disciple!"

The sangat hummed songs. As the sweet sounds of shabad filled my heart, I closed my eyes and pictured our previous Guru's fearless devotion to Sikhism—he sacrificed his life so we would be free. I marveled at the five fearless Sikhs who were willing to offer themselves to the Guru without question or doubt. If they could be that strong, so could I—even if I was a woman. My mind filled with peace.

The newly anointed panj pyare prepared a batch of blessed water for the entire congregation. They moved quickly, offering amrit to each willing Sikh. Soon, it was my turn.

Nectar was splashed over my head and eyes five times, and I felt a moment of jubilation as beads of water dripped down my face. I imagined them to be drops of sweat that would erupt from my forehead as I mastered my sword-handling skills.

At the end of the ceremony, we were served karah parshad as a blessing. I devoured the buttery, almond-colored sweet, licking the ghee off my palms. My mother, embarrassed by my unseemly behavior, elbowed me in the ribs. I didn't care. My veere had consumed their share with gusto. If my brothers could eat like wild animals, so could I. Parshad—a treat made of equal parts wheat, sugar, and ghee—embodied the message that we were all equal in the eyes of Waheguru.

"I am going outside to find our panj kakaar," said Dilbagh, gesturing to Chotu and me to follow.

People streamed from the tent. We weaved through the bustling crowds, trying to stay together. A group of girls giggled as they walked past my brothers. One of the kuriyaan smiled shyly at Chotu and whispered something to her friend. My brother kept a straight face, but as he walked away, he managed a sidelong look.

"Oy, you have an admirer." I laughed and nudged my veer.

Dilbagh snorted. "I can't imagine why."

Chotu ignored us, but his cheeks reddened. He quickly changed the subject. "My heart felt like it was going to burst when the Guru asked for a head!" he said, thumping his chest for effect.

"We owe our freedom to the Guru. We live in dangerous times, and our village could come under attack any day. We must be courageous and willing to die for others. I understand why the Guru asked the sangat for volunteers today," Dilbagh raised his voice.

"I agree with you. For once," I said, trying not to smile. He looked so proud.

"Pagal! You're holding the kirpan like a pail. It isn't used to fetch water from the well," a boy in blue clothes jeered at his friend. His friend slugged him in the arm.

"Did you see how the Guru's white falcon sat so quietly on his arm? So tame." An oval-faced aunty's jaw slackened in amazement.

I pointed to a group of Sikhs wearing the five symbols of our faith as ordained by the Guru, the panj kakaar.

"We're here, veere."

We approached a man handing out karas. I raised my right hand and slid the kara over my fingers to rest on my bare wrist. The bracelet glinted in the sunlight. *This kara represents my devotion to the One Light and my promise to uphold my dharam.*

A familiar smell brought back memories. As I turned to look, a brisk wind picked up the leaves by my feet and blew them toward a burly-looking man nearby. My eyes opened wide. A blacksmith! He held a red-hot kirpan in his hand, hammering and shaping it with a heavy tool. Sparks flew everywhere. I stood watching him work, my mouth agape.

My brothers nudged me, and I recovered myself.

"Sat Sri Akal." I pressed my hands together in respect.

He nodded and gravely handed us a kirpan each from his display of finely crafted weapons. The weight of the sword in my hands sent a shiver through me. *Do you know the significance of this blade? A kirpan is a blessing, a symbol of honor and self-respect. It is the defender of truth.* I understood, as a Sikh, I was only to use the kirpan in self-defense, when all other methods to restore peace had failed.

I squeezed Chotu's hand in excitement. I had my very own kirpan! It radiated energy, as though it had been fashioned from the brilliant rays of the sun. The silvery metal was warm to the touch. The hilt was bound with buffalo leather, functional yet elegant. The blade itself was the length of my arm and gently curved.

I gripped it in my right hand and tested it with the apprehension of a novice.

Dilbagh nudged me, bringing me out of my trance. "Let's go, Bhenji."

A big-bellied Sikh handed my brothers a length of cloth and a comb to help tie a dastaar, a turban. Tiny goose bumps pricked my arms. I, too, wanted to wear a dastaar. "I would like one, please." *Would he say no?*

Without a moment of hesitation, he placed the fabric and comb in my hands. "Here you are, Dhi." Grateful, I smiled at him. He nodded his head and moved to the next person in line.

"Bhenji, come with me," said Chotu, beckoning me to move to a more secluded area. My brothers were going to help tie my dastaar. My hair was already in a bun. Chotu and Dilbagh circled me solemnly, wrapping the cloth around my head with a firm hand. They did this in silence, the three of us deeply aware of the spiritual significance of this act. Chotu tucked the wooden comb into the last fold to secure everything in place.

My dastaar. I finally felt like my true self.

I threw my arms around my veere and squeezed them as tightly as I could. "Thank you."

"You've always been strong, but now you look it," said Chotu, beaming at me. Dilbagh was quiet.

"I will be back. I need to look at myself," I exclaimed, and rushed to find my way to the river. Standing at the edge of the calm waters of the Sutlej, I looked down at my reflection. I liked what I saw. Most women equated beauty with silky, cascading tresses covered by delicate chunnis. But I looked different. I looked powerful. *Will I be accepted?*

Just then, two women from the sangat arrived. They looked at me curiously, taking in my turban. One of them shed her clothes and walked into the water to bathe. Utterly comfortable in her round-bodied nakedness, she taught me a lesson: I, too, should shed any last feeling of unease about how I looked and revel in my new appearance. That day, I renounced that age-old feminine ideal of beauty. This dastaar, this symbol of my devotion, made me feel beautiful.

# EIGHT

The Guru's words continued to echo within me during the rest of our stay in Anandpur Sahib. *I have to stay and help. This is my dharam.*

When it was time to return home, I begged my father, "Pitaji, please allow me to remain with the Guru. I will learn to fight. Allow me to volunteer like the panj pyare did."

My father looked away, his eyes unfocused. "Again, Bhag Kaur? The battlefield is no place for you. You have been blessed, and you must spread these blessings back home. Come, we must go now."

His words lit a fire in me. I wanted to lash out at him, but I held my tongue. Did Pitaji not realize that I, too, was a descendant of the man who served in the armies of the sixth Guru? That I was as courageous and devoted as the men in my family? When would he open his eyes to truly see me for who I was?

During the long journey back to our village, I focused on my anger. I did not allow sore feet and aching legs to distract me. My resolve had now thickened like sugarcane juice boiled down to molasses. I urged my family homeward. I knew what I had to do.

Back in Jhabal Kalan, I was up before sunrise. I dressed in the blue robe of a Khalsa warrior and wrapped a saffron-colored dastaar around my head. Finally, I strung my kirpan over my chest and retrieved Pitaji's shield and other weapons from their hiding place. I was going to carry them to a spot outside, but lifting all that metal proved to be more challenging than I thought. I stumbled and dropped the shield. Almost immediately, my father appeared in the doorway.

"Pitaji. You did not allow me to train in Anandpur Sahib, so I will teach myself right here in Jhabal Kalan," I said, feigning bravery.

"You will do no such thing. You are not allowed to touch my weapons."

"I have my own sword now."

Pitaji eyed my kirpan. "That weapon is not to be used without the necessary training."

"But you won't teach me, so how can I learn? And so, I must teach myself."

Pitaji looked hurt and spoke in a soft voice, "I just do not understand why you are not like the other kuriyaan in the village."

"I am who I am. Will you teach me or not?"

My pitaji rested his hands on his thighs and looked at me for a long time. *Is he thinking of how to punish me?*

"I see your determination. Let me be clear, this does not mean you can sign up to fight. I will train you. This way, I can teach you how to use your weapon without injuring yourself."

"I accept!" I felt a rush of excitement flood my body.

My training began that day. "Bhag Kaur, you are about to learn shastar vidya, the science of weapons. The most important skill you will learn is deception. The blows your enemy doesn't see coming do the most damage."

Pitaji continued, "There are two types of combat— unarmed and armed. We will begin with learning how to correctly mount your horse, after which we will work on your unarmed combat skills. Ready, Dhi?"

"I am ready." I stood straight, trying hard to look like a real warrior.

Pitaji untied Kachu and walked her over to me. I loved this horse. I had spent many hours tending to her—feeding her hay, bathing her, and nourishing her with precious water. We had little of the life-sustaining liquid ourselves, but we were never stingy with the horses. My father believed that in order to ride a horse, you needed to learn to care for it first.

I knew how to ride Kachu, but with a kirpan strung over my body and a spear and a shield in each hand, mounting her proved challenging.

"You know there is little time to waste in combat. You must mount your horse faster." A look of irritation flashed across Pitaji's face.

"I am trying, but it is not easy with this extra weight." I gripped the saddle and pushed myself higher, only to lose my balance and crash to the ground. Kachu neighed her disapproval. I stood up and rubbed my sore bottom, thankful I wasn't speared.

After what felt like a thousand tries, I managed to mount Kachu in one smooth motion. Soon, the steady sound of her hooves filled the air, accompanied by the gentle swishing of her tail. I felt invigorated—I had mastered my first lesson.

Pitaji smiled for the first time that morning. "You've ridden well, Dhi. Let's stop for now. We will continue our lessons tomorrow." My sore, aching body welcomed the announcement. I slept early that night. Exhaustion delivered me almost immediately into sleep's gentle arms.

Before daylight, I was awake and alert, thirsty for more lessons. I joined my father and brothers in front of the house.

"Today, the four of us will focus on unarmed combat." Pitaji nodded at our eager faces.

He began by demonstrating how to brace ourselves for an attack. "Stand with your legs as wide apart as your hips—like this. And cross your arms over your chest, keeping them loose and ready to move."

My veere and I mimicked him, and he corrected us—my legs were too far apart, Chotu's too close, and Dilbagh had positioned his arms incorrectly. After we perfected our stance, we learned to punch with our fists, hit with our palms, and jab with our fingers. I'd wrestled since I was young, so this aspect of my training came with ease. Pitaji taught me how to launch into a perfect kick. I mastered elbow-attacks, knee-strikes, headbutts, chokeholds, body throws, and ground-fighting moves. Practice was intense, and it required immense focus and strength.

One morning, early on in our training, Dilbagh and I wrestled. I swung my fist at my tree-trunk-armed veer, and he jabbed me in return. Two blows from his knees and one headbutt later, I fell to the ground. Dilbagh pressed his heavy foot into my torso to signify defeat, throwing his hands in the air and basking in victory.

I lay in the dirt, my arms wrapped around me, writhing in pain. "Oyyyyy, it hurts so bad."

"Dhi, do you want to become a warrior or not? You must push yourself further than you imagined possible." Pitaji's brusqueness surprised me.

"Yes, Pitaji. I want to be a warrior—the best warrior I can be." Inside, I was seething at Dilbagh, and anger gave me the courage to stand up.

Pitaji continued to push us to our limits. I focused on my lessons with the concentration of a hungry animal stalking its prey. Most days, I was so sore, I could scarcely do my chores. A pail of water wearied my arms, and my legs trembled with every step.

But my body transformed as I trained. Though I was always strong, I developed more prominent muscles on my shoulders and arms. My thighs had a line of definition down the side, and my calves bulged with steel balls of muscle. My stomach was flat enough to rest a cup of water on it. I stood tall. And, as if it were possible, my physical strength couldn't compare to the growing strength of my will. My veere now struggled to defeat me in hand-to-hand combat. My mind raced back to the day Dilbagh took me down with ease. *Never again.*

One afternoon, I challenged Chotu. "Take your stance, bachcha. Prepare to lose."

"Use the moves I taught you, play to your individual strengths, and do so without compromising your dignity. We fight with integrity first," said Pitaji, moving away to allow us ample space.

We faced each other. I launched into a perfect kick and knocked Chotu down. He got up quickly and jabbed me in my face.

"Ah!" I rubbed my throbbing nose. I shook it off and charged at him with all my strength.

Chotu was taller than me and nimbly avoided my attack, but we collided before he could dart away. We tumbled to the ground, struggling for dominance. He managed to get on top of me and pinned my hands down. I promptly kneed him in the stomach, and he tumbled.

I hopped up and slammed my foot down on him. "Jit gaye!" Victory was mine!

Chotu jeered at me as he clutched his torso, "You look like a man!"

"You do look like a man," echoed Dilbagh.

Pitaji caught my eye and shook his head. I took the hint and ignored my ridiculous veere.

Mataji watched us from the threshold to our home, looking concerned. I could almost hear her thoughts. *I only want life to be easy for you, but your bullheaded personality makes that dream almost impossible.*

After one full moon cycle, Pitaji moved on to armed combat. It was going to be just the two of us.

He gestured at my kirpan strapped around my body. "Gurdas introduced you to wooden swords, which I know you are skilled at using. We will use our steel blades now."

I looked at him in consternation and then lowered my eyes. "I haven't had much practice with the kirpan. I am afraid I will hurt you with this."

Pitaji placed his index finger under my chin and lifted my head. "Bhag Kaur, raise your eyes and never lower them again. Courage springs from fear." Pitaji took a deep breath and went on, "You have the instincts of a warrior. I did not think it possible for a kuri, but you proved me wrong. A true soldier has complete control over their weapon. You will not hurt me. You will not allow yourself to."

*Oy, Pitaji believes in me!* I weighed the metal sword in my right hand and slashed the air in front of me. Sunlight bounced off the cool steel surface of the blade. "You say I won't hurt you, but this tip," —I poked the top of the kirpan— "is intended to pierce the flesh and kill."

"That is one way of looking at it. Another way to describe it would be that the sword is intended to defend innocent lives."

Pitaji moved on. "I need you to grasp the kirpan in one hand and imagine you are holding the wooden sword. The metal sword is the same weight as that wooden sword, no heavier. In the way that you know how to maneuver that wooden sword, you also know how to maneuver this kirpan. It's all in your mind."

I closed my eyes and focused on the weight of the sword, pushing out all other thoughts. A flash of memory was followed by the sharp sting of pain. I could see the face of my first teacher—Gurdas Veer.

"The kirpan is an extension of your arm, of your body. You and the blade are one and the same." Pitaji circled me as he spoke.

I imagined the sword attached to my body. I waved my arm, and the blade moved in sync. I raised the heavy weapon above my head and surprised myself at the ease with which I lifted it. Comfortable with the weight in my hand, I opened my eyes and crossed swords with my father. After that, Pitaji and I practiced regularly. The infinite possibilities of a single weapon astounded and humbled me. I steadily grew more proficient with each passing day.

One morning, Kulwinder Singh approached our house with his mother in the lead. His mataji scoffed when she saw me, clearly unimpressed by my skills. Kulwinder, on the other hand, stared at me with a strange look. I felt embarrassed. As a child, he looked at me with disdain when I wrestled him to the ground, but now, there was hunger in his eyes. The feeling was not mutual.

I ignored him and prepared to duel with my father.

"Take your position. Let's begin," said Pitaji, smiling.

I blocked Pitaji's feints, and he mine. We switched hands to mimic fighting with a double-edged khanda. The thrill I felt was all-encompassing.

"You are truly my dhi, nimble and powerful," Pitaji paid me a rare compliment as we sparred. "And don't worry that you might be smaller than your male opponent. A smaller target is harder to bring down. And if you move first, you can control your enemy."

We stopped when we noticed our guests were leaving not moments after they had arrived. Why had they come in the first place? Kulwinder hung his head low while his mataji scowled at me, her eyes bulging like a toad. She mumbled under her breath as she stormed off.

Wrapping up the day's practice, Pitaji said, "Dhi, always remember this—the battlefield is your holy ground. The double-edged sword is your prayer. Combat is your service. And victory is your karma."

I repeated the words to myself. Little did I know that these words, like a wave crashing upon the shore, would one day provide solace when I lay trapped in death's suffocating grasp.

I continued to train with my father for many moons and mastered the use of different weapons. Pitaji introduced me to a six-winged shispar mace, and I perfected striking blows with it. He taught me to use the three-pronged trishul, the weapon of choice of Shiva. Hurling a lasso, shooting with bows and arrows—he pushed me hard until I could wield each one with skill. It was the only time when my mind felt free, like a hawk soaring in the sky.

Pitaji described Sikh armor. "The Guru's chosen color for his fighters is blue, known as Khalsa Swarupa. Warriors wear sharp-edged bracelets called jangi kara. They carry the kirpan, and when dressed in full combat gear, a Sikh also carries two other swords: the curved talwar or the straight khanda on his hip—"

"Or hers," I interrupted.

"Yes, or hers. The second blade is a dagger called a katar on the left hip. On the back, the warrior wears a shield made from buffalo hide known as a dhala."

Pitaji held out an iron disk. "Dhi, this is a chakram, and this can be used to slice your opponent. We wear chakram on our arms and around our necks. Our turbans are reinforced with these disks to offer protection, so there is no need for any other form of headgear. We also sport an iron claw, a bagh naka, or a trident, a chand torra, hidden in our special dastaars to stab at close quarters." Pitaji paused and allowed me a moment to process all this information. I nodded for him to continue. "In times of war, Bhag Kaur, you reserve the weapons you are wearing. Only if you lose the weapon you are wielding, such as a sword, bow, or spear, would you use these. Our armor consists of chaar aina, a four-piece metal plate worn over chainmail. Our footwear is known as jangi mozeh, shoes with iron caps at the toe, capable of inflicting cuts and stab wounds."

My head was swimming. I realized I had only learned a fraction of what he could teach me, and this knowledge kept me humble. Like a potter, my pitaji was molding a warrior from a village kuri. "How will I retain all of your teachings?"

"Just as a simmer comes to a boil, learning is gradual."
Pitaji then demonstrated a strike with his trident-topped turban. He lowered his head parallel to the ground, his eyes raised. Then he pulled his head back with great force and thrust it forward to stab his imaginary opponent. I practiced the move multiple times.

Pitaji then handed me a sword, and we sparred again. He slashed toward my left.

"Not today, death," I said, swiftly blocking his swing. I quickly regrouped, but Pitaji was unprepared. He fell to the ground, looking up at me in amazement. I took a step back.

"Did you fall on purpose, Pitaji?" I was unable to conceal my surprise.

Pitaji stood up and dusted off his clothes. "No, Dhi, you defeated me." He then turned and walked away in the direction of our home.

Did he leave because the lesson was over for the day? Or did his defeat mean more?

That evening, I rushed to find Jeeti. I was carrying my sheathed kirpan, as the Guru had instructed us to do. She wasn't at home, so I went to look for her in the fields where she liked to talk to her friends. I wanted to speak to her about my pitaji's defeat that morning. But she wasn't there, either.

"Ahhhhhhh, stop!" It was Jeeti's voice!

I sprinted in the direction of the sound, my heart beating against my chest in panic.

A much older man had pinned her against the tree. Her clothes were ripped, and she was flailing her arms. Bile rose to my mouth. The pervert turned around when he heard me. He looked down his beaked nose before facing Jeeti again.

"Leave her alone."

The man pretended not to hear me. I unsheathed my kirpan. "If you value your life, I suggest you leave. Now!"

Fear nipped at my mind—this was my first real attack. Sweat rolled down my face in fat, salty beads. The man turned around in shock. I gripped my blade and positioned myself for a fight.

"Little girl, put that weapon down before you hurt yourself," he said, his words laced with scorn. He pulled out a dagger from under his kurta and waved it at me, swaying from side to side as if he were drunk.

"I don't know where you've come from, but you are in our village. We are warriors in Jhabal Kalan. If you don't leave, you will die by my hand," I said with conviction as I lunged forward in his direction.

He paused, and fear flashed across his face. *Had he been faking bravado?* The man snarled and made a move toward me. Then, much to my surprise, he slid the dagger back into his garments and stormed off. It hadn't been an actual fight, but I protected my cousin with my kirpan. I thanked Waheguru.

Jeeti was sobbing by the tree, trying to wrap her torn clothing around her. Her chunni had fallen to the ground, and her hair was disheveled. I rushed to her and folded her into my arms. She was shaking in terror. Her sobs broke through like a river crashing through a dam. I held her until she calmed down.

"Jeeti, I hate that this happened to you. You didn't deserve this."

"Let's not allow hate to fill our hearts. You came just in time to save me. I was wrong—you are truly a great warrior, my bhen." Jeeti squeezed my hand.

I looked into her dark eyes, still wet with tears. "Jeeti, who was that man?"

"I don't know. I came here to find my friends, when he came out of the woods. I've never seen him in our village." Jeeti stared into the distance. "Do not tell anyone about what happened. Vaada karo. Even if it was not my fault, you know what people will say. I will be blamed for his actions, and no one will marry me."

My heart ached for her. "You have my word. But if I see him again, I will kill him. That is also a promise."

# NINE

The following morning, I ate breakfast in silence, mulling over the events of the day before. Once I finished eating, I walked over to my father, who was meditating.

"Pitaji, you are not training me today?"

"Dhi, you are a trained warrior. From now on, you must practice what I have taught you. Speak to your mataji. She has something important to tell you."

I ran to my mataji. "My training is complete, Mataji! Can you believe it?"

Mataji smiled. "Dhi, we have some good news." She flipped a roti, which puffed up on the heat of the chulha. "We found you a husband. He is a good Sikh. A warrior, like you."

I felt like cold water had been poured over me. A past conversation with Jeeti came back to me. "*One day, we will be married with families and homes of our own, Bhen. Isn't the thought exciting?*"

I remembered the other kuriyaan in the village chattering about their futures and who they secretly wished their husbands would be. I understood the importance of marriage and family, even as I struggled to imagine sharing my home, my meals, and my bed with a stranger.

Mataji ignored my stunned expression and went on, "His name is Nidhan Singh, and he is from Patti. Their village is not far from here. He comes from a respectable family—landowners. You will like him."

Did owning land equate to being a good person? Would a man raised by a respectable family love and respect me? My mataji shared more details, but my mind drifted. What about my dream? If I got married, any chance I had of setting off to the battlefield was gone forever. A woman, let alone a wife, could not fight in a war. What if my husband did not want me to practice my new skills? My stomach lurched.

"You know, Kulwinder and that difficult woman, his mother, came to ask for your hand," Mataji muttered.

I snorted, momentarily distracted. Kulwinder Singh, my nemesis, wanted to marry me?

"She strode in with such entitlement and said her puttar sought your hand in marriage. But she would not accept a daughter-in-law who engaged in manly pursuits. She thought I would agree, and she stood there waiting. Bhag Kaur, what do you think I said? I told her, 'Then you won't have a daughter-in-law from this house. Find someone else for your son.' She stormed out, calling us a strange family who would be lucky to have her puttar as a groom. Kulwinder looked mortified. I would never let you marry a man who cowered behind his mataji's chunni the way he did. On the other hand, Nidhan Singh is a good man."

I didn't respond. I could never dishonor my parents by refusing this match. They must have gone to great lengths to find a suitable groom. After all, I wasn't a typical kuri. A wave of guilt washed over me.

Mataji looked at me, obviously displeased. "You will need to wear proper clothes for the wedding. None of these warrior outfits you wear. Do you hear me, Bhag Kaur?"

"Mataji, what about my practice?" I asked. "You know I spent all this time sparring with Pitaji. As a wife, I won't be allowed to continue, and it will kill me if I have to stop."

"I told his mother about your battle training, even though I feared they would decline your hand. She spoke to her son, and he found you intriguing." It must have taken courage for Mataji to be honest with his mother.

Suddenly, I couldn't breathe. I ran outside for air.

"Bhag Kaur!" Mataji yelled, begging me to stop.

"Ahhhh!" I emptied my lungs, feeling helpless and lost.

I needed to find Jeeti.

Jeeti's warm smile momentarily pacified me. "What's wrong?"

Above us, leaves rustled in the wind. We were surrounded by shrubbery dotted with white flowers, obstructing our view of our homes.

"Why do you want to get married?" I asked.

"I want to build a home of my own. Have a grand wedding that culminates in the union of two hearts beating as one. I imagine our relationship to blossom like a flower with radiant petals unfurling in the warmth of the sun."

Tears rolled down my face. "I knew this day would come, but why am I not happy? My family has arranged my marriage to a man named Nidhan Singh. But Jeeti, unlike you, I am scared and angry."

"But if you didn't marry, then what? You'd prefer to die never having known love?" Jeeti asked.

"Yes, if my sacrifice saves lives. I truly believe in the Guru's call to action. I can feel it more strongly now."

"You must trust your parents to do what is right. Perhaps you can have both." With those words, Jeeti walked back to her house.

I returned home to find my mother sitting outside on a manji. A sudden rush of understanding flooded me. "There will be no dowry, Mataji."

"We will see." A flicker of pride lit up her eyes. "Dhi, just like you plant a seed and water it with love, so shall your relationship grow. You will learn."

"Hanji, Mataji," I gave in to her wishes.

In the days leading up to my wedding, the house was alive with joyous preparations. Every nook and cranny was dusted; every vessel polished. The women ground dried corn and harvested mustard greens and onions. They prepared mitai, sweets of every shape and color.

My mouth watered at the sight of the boondi laddoo, balls of chickpea flour deep-fried and soaked in syrupy-sweet liquid. I attempted to sneak a yellow laddoo from under the watchful eyes of my mother and aunt. Mataji promptly smacked my hand. "Those are for the wedding, greedy girl."

Mamiji and Mataji were embroidering a beautiful wedding shawl, a phulkari bagh, for me. My mother hummed a folk tune as she stitched. Mamiji and I joined in. "Ih phulkari meri maan ne kadhi. Is noo ghut japhiyan paawan." This phulkari was embroidered by my mataji, and I embrace it warmly.

The bagh was designed to reflect the beauty of our land. Wheat and barley stalks laid out in neat geometric patterns covered the expanse of fabric, golden crops undulating against rich brown earth. It was mesmerizing in its detail. On the day of the wedding, I'd drape the bagh around me and wrap myself in their love.

"Satleen Kaur just got married, and her bagh was not as beautiful as yours. You will look like royalty on the day," said Mamiji as she put the final touches on my luxurious gift.

I gave her a tight squeeze. Life had been hard on Mamiji, but she was never bitter. She continued to laugh and enjoy life. I hoped to be as strong of heart as she was.

One evening, the women had gathered to shape another batch of laddoos when the crunching of leaves underfoot alerted us to someone's arrival. Two women, followed by a young man, stood respectfully at the threshold of our home.

"Sat Sri Akal Ji," the man greeted my mother. "My mataji and bhenji wished to meet you before the wedding."

The young man was tall and well-built, with skin the color of the skies at dusk. Under his thick beard, I could make out a broad jawline and . . . dimples? I couldn't be sure.

I looked up, and our eyes met. *Nidhan Singh.*

His expression softened, and a flicker of interest danced in his eyes. My face flushed. Our eyes met again, but this time I lowered my eyes and quickly looked away. It occurred to me that he was using his family as cover, that he was hoping to catch a glimpse of me.

"Jee aaya nu," said Mataji, beaming from ear to ear as she welcomed them. "Please sit, and I will bring you something to eat. If you are looking for Uncleji, he is out in the fields."

"We have eaten, so please don't go to any trouble. We came to meet everyone. We will find Uncleji now." Nidhan Singh's eyes returned to me.

"Sat Sri Akal Ji," I said, pressing my hands together, and they returned the greeting.

The trio then turned and walked toward the fields. Mamiji elbowed me, and Mataji had a coy expression on her face. I grew hot with embarrassment and focused on forming a perfectly spherical laddoo.

He wasn't that bad . . .

That night, my family walked through our village in a jaago procession to invite our neighbors to attend the wedding celebrations. The women carried decorated clay pots topped with oil lamps to light the way. The raucous sounds of singing and peals of laughter lit up our little Jhabal Kalan.

At home, I stretched out on my manji to rest. I could hear the joyous cacophony from where I lay, and my heart filled with love. Each one of those loud, boisterous noisemakers out there cared for me dearly. I realized how lucky I had been to grow up here. I tried to memorize every detail of my childhood home—the cracks that crept across the walls, the roughness of the frayed ropes of the manji, the way the baskets my mother made would fit my hip, the shape of the mango tree in the courtyard, even the weight of the chipped clay dishes we ate off of every day. This house would be my refuge no longer.

Anxiety and fear swirled in my mind. *Would my husband and I grow to love one another? Would my in-laws care for me?* Panic seized me. *Breathe, Bhag Kaur.*

The wedding was to take place in front of my family's home. Our clan had gathered for the event, and all our neighbors were expected to attend.

My aunt and Jasmeet arrived early in matching golden-yellow salwar-kameez sets. Mamiji held a box in her hands. Inside, she had arranged row upon row of delicately ornamented ivory bangles: my churra.

Mamiji squatted by my side and lifted my right arm. I held my arm steady while she slid the red and ivory bangles over my wrist, one by one. With my entire forearm encased, she then moved to my left arm. These bangles were to remain on my arms for many moons as a blessing.

Mamiji patted my hands. "These look beautiful on you." She smiled, but I knew how she must be feeling. Following tradition, it would have been my uncle, my mamaji, who would have slid the churra onto my wrists.

"I miss them," I whispered.

"Their blessings are here with you today," she said with a watery smile.

"Auntyji, how did you find bangles large enough to fit Bhag Kaur's hands?" Jeeti teased, pinching my arm.

"There is a woman in the village who makes them. I showed her the size of Bhag Kaur's wrists with my fingers, like so," Mamiji spread the fingers of her right hand as wide as she could, laughing mischievously.

I was wearing a red salwar-kameez embroidered with intricate gold embroidery. *Red symbolizes prosperity and fertility.* My stunning phulkari bagh was wrapped around my shoulders, with one end draped over my head. At my hair part, I wore a teardrop-shaped gold ornament that grazed the top of my forehead. A gold hoop adorned my nose, and gold cascaded down my front in the form of a heavy necklace. My arms were stiff with ivory churra, and my fingers weighed down with rings. I had never seen such fine clothing and jewelry. It would have taken my parents many moons of bartering goods to secure these jewels for my wedding. *How can I question their wisdom when they love me this much?*

My mother rubbed a bit of ghee on my face and tinted my cheeks with juice from crushed betel leaves. "Just enough to enhance your natural beauty," Mataji declared, pleased with her handiwork.

Nidhan Singh arrived atop a horse. He was dressed in the electric blue robes of the Khalsa, crowned with a towering, perfectly symmetrical blue turban. Sehra, strands of white flowers, covered his chiseled face like a floral waterfall. He held a majestic kirpan in one hand. He made a striking groom. *Is he as nervous as I am?*

Once the groom's procession, the baraat, settled down, our families began the milni ceremony. Male members on both sides shared introductions while the women looked on. This was when I learned that Nidhan Singh's father had attained salvation in battle alongside our sixth Guru. Pitaji swapped a familial meeting with the groom's paternal uncle instead. After them, other family members partnered up, until everyone had been formally introduced, garlands had been exchanged, and blessings were spread around the congregation.

With my eyes trained on the ground, I made my way slowly toward the Holy Book, the Adi Granth. Jeeti and Jasmeet flanked me on either side and held my hands, their touch warming me. *Why am I shivering?*

Nidhan Singh sat in front, his family forming a semicircle behind him. An empty spot to his left was reserved for me. Sitting down, I caught my soon-to-be husband stealing a sideways glance at me. Was he smiling?

Wave upon wave of anxiety and guilt crashed upon me. This was a divine union of two souls, and I should feel elated. *Waheguru, help me understand.*

Bhai Sahib, the priest, began reciting the sacred wedding hymns, the lava phera, filling the morning air with praise for the Gurus. After each lava, Nidhan Singh and I stood up and circled the Adi Granth, united by a long piece of cloth that we both held.

Mataji looked regal in a guava-pink suit, her gauzy chunni resting obediently on her neat hair bun. Sitting by my side, she kept her eyes closed as she gently swayed in rhythm. My brothers' heads were lowered in respect. Tears streamed down Pitaji's cheeks and disappeared into his gray-black beard. The sight of his tears caused mixed feelings to swirl through my body like a whirlpool. In a few moments, I would be the wife of a stranger. I would never live with my parents again. I closed my eyes and prayed for guidance.

The fourth and final round around the Holy Book marked our spiritual union—we were wed. I turned to look at my husband, and he met my gaze. *Will you love me? And in time, will I be able to love you, too?*

After an exchange of gifts, our guests were served a special meal of makki ki roti and saag. At the end, we offered them the many varieties of sweets we spent days preparing. I had not eaten all day. I scooped up a laddoo and tried to shove it into my mouth discreetly. As soon as I did, I felt a pat on my arm and turned around to face my mother with puffy cheeks. She clucked her disapproval and shooed away the woman she was waiting to introduce me to.

I spotted Nidhan Singh walking toward me, and I swallowed the laddoo whole. He smiled with kind eyes, his dimples further softening his features. But before he could speak, my parents intercepted him, with Chotu and Dilbagh in tow.

Pitaji's eyes were bloodshot as he placed his hands on the tops of our heads to bless us. Then, he pulled us closer together. "May Waheguru bless you both for eternity."

"I will miss you. I promise to write," Chotu said.

I didn't want to go just yet. "Take care of Mataji and Pitaji."

Dilbagh puffed his chest and said, "I'll take care of the weapons, don't worry. We will miss you, Bhenji." I gave my tough veer a tight hug.

"Dhi, do not worry about us. It is time for you to make your home," said Mataji, shifting awkwardly and forcing a smile. Pitaji placed his hand on the small of her back, a rare affectionate touch.

I did what I thought they would have wanted: I did not cry. I could see some of my relatives' eyes widen as they placed their hands over their mouths. *A bride not crying at her farewell ceremony. Besharam! Shameless!* At that moment, no one mattered to me more than my mother, so I ignored them. I hugged my mataji tight. Had she felt me trembling?

Nidhan Singh's family had gathered, ready to make the half-day journey south to their home in Patti. Dutifully, I walked up to Nidhan Singh, who took my hand and gently tugged me toward him. There was warmth in his touch, but I felt uncomfortable.

"Soni lagdi." You look beautiful. Two simple words filled me with not-so-simple emotions. *He seems kind.*

My veere hoisted me onto the doli, my palanquin. I nearly toppled over, but Dilbagh caught my shoulder and pushed me inward. After I was seated, Chotu interlocked his fingers and created a step for Nidhan Singh to climb onto the platform. He reached out for my hand to help pull him up, and I hesitantly obliged. Suddenly aware of our onlookers, I realized we must have looked like royalty as we began the journey to my new home.

# TEN

"We are home." Nidhan Singh prompted the men carrying our palanquin to set us down. Once we were on the ground, our bearers unloaded my belongings and helped us alight.

A vast field of golden-eared wheat swayed in the wind. A cool breeze picked up, and I inhaled deeply. The familiar scent of rich earth filled my nostrils, calming me. At a distance, I spotted a house. My family owned a fair amount of land, but this was more land for one family than I had seen. Mataji was right. *Wonderful! I can practice in peace, I won't have to deal with prying neighbors and curious village kids.*

The palanquin bearers ambled off, leaving the two of us with my mother-in-law. My sister-in-law lived in Amritsar with her family, so it was just the three of us now. This was going to be my new home in Patti, and I had to live with two people I barely knew. I felt like a guest.

Nidhan Singh's mataji walked ahead to give us some privacy while my husband scooped up the baskets containing my few belongings.

"These are our wheat fields, and we grow vegetables in these beds on our right. We have four cows and three horses. The family well is just outside our home," said Nidhan Singh, pointing to things that I could see for myself.

"Ma enjoys cooking, and she takes pride in it." He glanced at me. "She loves to be complimented. Otherwise, she doesn't talk much since my pitaji's passing."

*Our community has lost so many good men. Appreciate what you have, Bhag Kaur.*

I hadn't spoken since we had left my village, and I wondered if Nidhan Singh had noticed, when he spoke again. "Are you nervous? Marriage is a big change, especially for you." He stopped in front of the doorway, blocking my path. I thought I saw a flash of a smile.

"Yes," I said flatly. "I have left my home and family behind." He looked confused and hurt, so I tried to make up for my lack of enthusiasm by adding, "It is my dharam to make this my home, and I will." But deep down, I was unsure if I truly could.

"May we go in?"

He must have sensed my hesitation. He promptly moved away from the doorway to allow me to enter, but I stood there, frozen.

Similar to my home in Jhabal Kalan, the house was constructed of solid bricks, though the construction was newer and the home larger.

His mataji appeared with a clay pot filled with water and a dish mounded with flour and sat down. She raised her eyes to look at me but didn't say a word. She began kneading the flour into dough with gusto. Like my mataji, she wore her hair pulled back into a tight bun on the top of her head; her earth-colored chunni covered her hair and framed her face. She had small features, and her soft eyes creased at the corners. From under her chunni, I noticed she had an almost perfect distribution of silver and black hair, giving her a distinctive look. She reminded me of my own mother. *She seems kind.*

"Look around the house," said Nidhan Singh as he went inside. "I can put your belongings away." I followed him into a large room that served as the common space. Another room opened to the right, with four manji arranged in a neat row. Nidhan Singh set my baskets down next to one of the cots.

"Please leave my things there. I will unpack them."

The first night in my new home, I kept twisting and turning in a futile attempt to relax. Nidhan Singh was asleep next to me, snoring like a lion. I watched his chest rise and fall, resenting his peaceful face as I wriggled around, desperately banging on sleep's door.

The following morning, my eyelids felt like they were being weighed down by bricks. Nidhan Singh looked at me kindly but said nothing. I shifted uncomfortably as he watched me rub the crusts out of my eyes and smooth out my tangled hair. Up until a few days ago, I'd never even met the man, and now we were waking up next to each other. Soon enough, I would have to fulfill my duty to him as his wife. The thought terrified me. *You are a warrior, and you are afraid of being a dutiful wife?*

"Ma made fresh parate. Are you hungry?" asked Nidhan Singh, bringing me back to the present. My husband had tied a red dastaar and groomed his thick beard before he woke me. He wore a white kurta-pajama, which highlighted his muscular frame.

Once we were outside, his mother gestured to the food and retreated into the home. We ate in silence. The savory parate reminded me of my mataji's, and the familiar flavors of home eased some of my tension.

Nidhan Singh appeared uncomfortable, twisting his hands together as he spoke. "It must be difficult adjusting to a new family." His voice was deep but soft, not unlike my pitaji's.

"It is," I tried to be polite. After all, I was going to live with him for the rest of my life. But the knot in my stomach would not release. I never had trouble making conversation before. I knew I had to try, even if a part of me rebelled against it. "Your mother's cooking is delicious, much like my mataji's. After this meal, I feel more at home here." My husband's back straightened, and he looked relieved.

We took a walk after our meal. Nidhan Singh pointed out some of his favorite places—the mango tree he climbed as a child, the storage area behind the home where he preserved his father's weapons, and a quiet escape beside a tiny stream. We stopped to rest beneath a banyan tree, its leathery leaves glistening above our heads. Below, crimson blossoms dotted a long row of shrubs, tiny floral flames bursting through a wall of greenery. Lulled by the gentle sounds of flowing water, I was afraid I might fall asleep, and drew circles in the dirt to keep my eyes open. I thought of the Sutlej River in Anandpur Sahib, where I'd felt beautiful and complete.

"What do you think of this place?" asked Nidhan Singh, resting his hand on a tree root. He probably thought I was thinking about him.

"This is peaceful. I can see why you come here."

Nidhan Singh glanced at me with a flicker of interest, but I averted my gaze. Blushing, I stood up and took a few wobbly steps toward the water. He offered his hand, but I brushed it away.

"Are you feeling well?"

"Yes, I am. Sorry . . . it's just that my thoughts drifted."

His eyes searched mine, desperate to be let in.

It took nearly twenty nights before I was able to calm myself enough to be able to sleep. Revived after a full night's sleep, I was feeling cheerful. I even managed to smile at my husband. A plate of hot food was in front of him, but he sat alone.

"Where's Ma?"

"Off on her morning walk." Nidhan Singh turned his attention to his meal. "Join me?" He patted the ground next to him.

I made up a plate and sat across from him instead.

"I don't carry any disease. If you sat by me and your leg were to touch mine accidentally, you would not die." He rose in anger, and his plate flipped over, his breakfast scattering.

I pulled back instinctually, my heart skipping a beat. I had hurt him deeply.

Nidhan Singh disappeared the rest of the day—I knew he was avoiding me. *What if he sends me back to Jhabal Kalan? I'll bring shame to my family.*

The sun was about to set—still no sign of him. I rolled out rotis for the evening meal, and his mother flipped them over the chulha.

"Where do you think he went, Ma?"

Ma looked at me for a moment and returned to the roti she was flipping. "Tilling the fields or chopping wood."

I couldn't read her expressionless face. "Do you think he will return while the food is still hot?"

Ma tilted her head to the side but said nothing.

We spent the evening in complete silence. "Ma, I am going for a walk. Will you give him his dinner when he returns?"

She nodded.

Once I was far from the house, I drew my kirpan from its sheath. The setting sun set the sky on fire—a battle cry to rally the moon and stars against the gathering darkness. I reached down and touched my toes, followed by a series of stretches to wake up my body. Warmed up, I lunged forward and sliced my sword through the air with a magnificent whoosh, then stepped back and crossed my sword across my chest to deflect an imaginary counter-attack. I jabbed, then pivoted and lunged in the opposite direction. Soon, I was completely at peace, one with my weapon.

I didn't see Nidhan Singh coming, but the sound of grass crunching underfoot made me look around. He was dressed in a fresh, cream-colored kurta-pajama, the thin cloth sticking to his torso and outlining his firm body. His long hair cascaded down his shoulders in waves, dripping water at the tips. He must have taken a dip in the stream.

He walked up to me, stopping less than a foot away from me. "Ma said you were looking for me." As he met my gaze, defiance flashed across his face. He was daring me to challenge him.

My palms moistened with sweat. "You were gone the whole day, and I thought you might be hungry. Have you eaten?"

He nodded wordlessly, and I felt the sting of rejection.

I kept talking, suddenly very aware of our proximity. "Ever since that Baisakhi day at Anandpur Sahib, I have wanted to answer the Guru's call to fight. Our men are brave but severely outnumbered in this unjust war. I have trained under my pitaji, and practice is important to me. This kirpan is my most treasured possession." Nervous, my hands flew to my disheveled hair, and I attempted to smooth out my chunni. I hadn't tied my dastaar that morning.

"When Ma brought up your sword-fighting skills, I was intrigued," Nidhan Singh said, watching me with interest.

"Were you? I was nervous you'd find it odd."

"Not at all. I find it attractive." A shy grin spread across his face. "I have a special gift for you." He reached into a satchel and pulled out a double-edged sword—a khanda.

"Dilbagh told me that you have only a kirpan of your own. I wanted to gift you your second weapon." With his head held high, he handed me the heavy blade, but I couldn't get a good grip and dropped it.

Nidhan Singh looked crushed. "It is too heavy for you. Don't worry, I will have a new one made for you. You will have every Khalsa weapon specially forged for you. That is my promise."

"Thank you. You are kind," I said, unsure of what to say next. *Make an effort, Bhag Kaur!*

I rattled on, "Growing up in a large, noisy family, I am used to a busy life. Here it is just the three of us, encircled by all this farmland. At times, I feel lonely, and I miss my family dearly." A firefly flew into his beard, and I brushed it away. "At home, I would voice my opinions even if my family didn't agree, but here I am not sure if that would be acceptable. But please know that I appreciate the kindness shown by you and your mataji."

"Please be yourself. I want to hear your thoughts and desires. This is your home, and you are my family." He hesitated for a moment and then whispered, "I love you."

My heart skipped a beat. I froze. *Say it back.*

Crestfallen, he continued, "I know I might always love you more, but your respect and kindness are all I need."

I took a deep breath, trying to form a reply, but he interrupted me, "You never have to say something you don't mean, Bhag Kaur. Love is to be given without the expectation of return." He turned his attention to weighing the khanda in his hands, relieving me of the obligation to respond.

This man, with his thoughtful demeanor and loving heart, deserved a happy marriage. His devotion was like a soothing balm, the faithful moon rising each night and bathing me in light. I hated myself for not caring for him more. But my heart eluded control. And, as cruel and illogical as it was, I felt angry at him. Why did he have to love me so much? Why wasn't he mad at me for not loving him enough?

Feeling guilty because I thwarted his attempt to romance me, and longing for those I loved, I felt a sudden urge to hold him close. I slipped my hand into his, and he stroked my hair. My skin tingled, and the warmth of his body next to mine enveloped me like an old blanket. I longed to wrap my arms around him, but I hesitated. *Is it appropriate for a woman to do so? What if he doesn't reciprocate?*

We stared at each other, unspoken words hanging in the air. The world around us faded away, and for one sweet moment, we were the only two people who mattered. I saw a hunger in his eyes, a hunger I felt as well.

"Bhag Kaur . . ." he whispered, hugging me, and my heart pulsed feverishly.

Breathless, I thirsted for more.

Just then, we heard the sound of leaves crunching. Ma appeared from behind us but didn't seem to have noticed anything. "Oy, it's getting dark. Are you both fine?"

"Yes, we are. We should go, Bhag Kaur." He let go, and the tiny, residual feeling of fingers coasting across my back tickled me after we separated.

# ELEVEN

In the morning, I spotted a distant figure moving near our fields. Nidhan Singh. He hadn't tied his dastaar, and his disheveled, curly hair rested on his shoulders in tiny ringlets. He waved an old sword in rapid swings, wearing only a loincloth wrapped carefully between his thighs. The lean muscles on his arms rippled as he moved; his deep amber-brown skin shone in the early light. My cheeks reddened.

I sneaked back inside and retrieved my kirpan. I slid a chunni over my head since I hadn't tied my turban. He watched me walk toward him. We stood close, and the faint scent of spices on his skin tickled my nose. Our eyes locked, and his temples glistened with sweat. His gaze hypnotized me, refusing to release me. Then, suddenly, he turned his face away. *Is he protecting himself?*

I slipped into a fighting stance and clasped the hilt of my sword, eyes glued on him. I waited for his move, my heart pounding in a way I'd never felt before.

He lunged forward and attempted to stab me in my chest. I blocked his thrust easily, and his sword crossed mine. He retreated, and I slashed at him, missing on purpose. I changed directions and swiped at his chest, stepping forward with my left foot. Nidhan Singh rocked backward and deflected my advance. My sword clanged against his, allowing him to advance on me. He pivoted with his left foot and then whipped around in a swift circle. I leaped backward and narrowly avoided the hit. We continued sparring, bold attacks and swift parries, both equally capable of holding the other off.

"You're quick," panted Nidhan Singh.

"You are strong," I replied, gasping for air.

The physical exertion required for swordplay left me fatigued. But I felt mentally invigorated, even exhilarated. My body tingled.

Nidhan Singh was glowing in the crimson light of the sun, his face dark with a wolflike craving. I leaped forward again, going low and aiming for his legs. He jumped up in a perfectly timed move, stepped back, and switched his sword to his right hand. He rushed toward me, sweeping his blade from the side toward my midriff. I blocked the strike with a twist of my hips.

I felt at ease with him, enjoying this new wordless connection as we engaged in swordplay. I wanted to spar all day, but my body betrayed me. My breath grew heavier, and sweat drenched my clothes. He squinted at me. Had he noticed that I was getting tired?

"You are a challenging opponent." He lowered his kirpan and grabbed my hand, pulling me toward him, a mischievous grin lighting up his face.

"Where are we going?" I struggled to keep up as he pulled me into the fields.

Stopping abruptly beneath the banyan tree, he shouted, "We are going to dance!"

He spun around in joy, his hands in the air. I laughed as he swayed his hips, singing a gloriously off-key folk song. As he moved, his body spoke to me. Usually guarded, he burst into the most vibrant version of himself in dance. With each move, it became painfully clear how deep his feelings for me ran. He turned, his eyes boring into me, head tilted to one side with a hopeful smile on his lips.

I started to dance. As I wiggled my body, I felt like my younger self, when life was free of sorrow and loss. I embraced him, letting him take control of my body. A world of love that I needed as badly as I needed to breathe woke within me.

We moved with unrestrained joy, unafraid of being discovered. To dance barefoot in the grass was a pleasure unknown to me, and I let my hair hang loose, my red chunni flying in the breeze.

It began drizzling, and we took shelter beneath the banyan tree. The rain fell softly, as if it knew of the hardships behind us and those to come. As each raindrop kissed our skin, they sang of treasured memories and comforting love.

Nidhan Singh laughed wildly as the water streamed through our hair and down my neck until it soaked our clothes. He jumped on top of me, and we rolled on the ground, limbs entangled. Impulsively, I pressed my wet lips against his and felt his body tense.

We pulled apart, panting in shallow breaths. Unable to contain himself anymore, Nidhan Singh held my face in his hands and pulled me into a fiery kiss. I ran my hands over his arms, feeling each bump and crevasse of his perfect physique.

We pulled apart, and I opened my eyes. We stared at each other; his eyes were full of wonder. The cool wind cut through me like a dagger, but I didn't care. I was overjoyed. The clouds grew darker, and the gentle pitter-patter of rain turned into a waterfall as the water cascaded to the ground, forcing us to return to the house.

Once inside, we watched the clouds part and let through a shaft of watery, white light—its brilliance setting the world alight.

The seasons passed, and one day a courier arrived bearing an invitation—Dilbagh was getting married. We set off for Jhabal Kalan that week to help with the preparations.

"Jee aaya nu! My dhi and puttar have arrived," exclaimed a beaming Mataji. She hugged us in turn.

"Come. We've set up a room for you, so Nidhan Singh is comfortable in our house."

"Where's Pitaji? And Chotu and Dilbagh?" I looked around.

"They've gone to the bazaar to buy fabric for new clothes. As the groom's family, we don't have much to do besides getting dressed." She smiled as she set a basket containing some of our belongings down near a manji.

The familiar smells of Mataji's cooking filled me with nostalgia. Everything looked the same, yet I felt different. This wasn't my residence any longer, but it was home.

A new mare was tied to one of the trees outside. "Mataji, I see a new horse tied to the tree outside. Where's Kachu?"

Mataji averted her eyes. "Dhi, she was old. Kachu lived a good life, and she is at peace now."

"What? Why didn't anyone tell me?" A memory of riding Kachu through our fields flashed through my mind, hitting me like a lightning bolt.

Nidhan Singh gently changed the topic. "Mataji, we are happy to see you."

"I am overjoyed that you both are here. What can I cook for you, Puttar? I will make your favorite foods. Just tell me what you like."

A prickle of annoyance flustered me. *I am here, too. What about my favorites?* "We can all eat roti with daal. I'll help you cook."

"Son, you get some rest. You've had a long journey." Mataji continued to address her son-in-law, patting the manji helpfully. Nidhan Singh obediently lay down on the cot, and Mataji and I walked outside toward the chulha.

"Dhi, why did you offer only roti and daal? My son-in-law is visiting us for the first time after the wedding. He deserves a feast for a king."

I worked the dough with unnecessary force. "You are my mataji, not his, or have you forgotten?" I snapped, regretting the words even before they escaped my mouth.

"You are my dhi, be sure of that. But he must know my love for him because he has not had a lifetime to experience it. My love is for you both, don't forget."

Mataji rinsed the daal in a clay vessel. She added, "Jeeti is with her family in Amritsar. She sent her regrets."

"I was hoping to see Jeeti." The dough stuck to my palms as I rolled out the pede, and I laughed to myself, remembering how Jeeti made perfect rotis and kept her hands clean.

"Her belly is swelling, which is why she cannot come. She looks even more beautiful as a mother-to-be, as if that is possible." Mataji pointedly looked at my stomach. "It is our dharam as women to bring children into the world."

Her words made me feel inadequate. "I am aware, Mataji. You will receive a letter if it happens."

"If?" Mataji's lips thinned, and she curled up her fingers like a lotus. "Dhi, there will be a bachcha. I will pray for one and the happiness it will bring you. Be strong and trust in Waheguru."

"Eh, Bhag Kaur!"

Chotu came running toward us with Pitaji and Dilbagh behind him. I dropped the dough ball I was shaping, grateful for the distraction.

Chotu wrapped his arms around my waist and spun me around in circles. "I am so happy to see you, Bhenji."

Dilbagh and Pitaji carried bales of fabric in their arms. They hugged me, and their familiar scent welcomed me home.

"Oy, Dilbagh, someone agreed to marry you? How did you manage that trick?" I squeezed my veer's arm.

"Oy, stop! Her name is Harleen Kaur. She is from our village. Her family moved here after you married," replied Dilbagh, looking annoyed.

Just then, Nidhan Singh walked out of the house. "Sat Sri Akal, Pitaji, veere, heartiest wishes on the wedding."

"Jee aaya nu. We are overjoyed you came early." Pitaji patted him on the back. "Has Bhag Kaur made you something to eat? Why aren't you resting?" *Will they stop fawning over their son-in-law?*

"She is preparing a meal. I did get some rest, but I am not that tired. Do not worry about me, please. Can you do me the honor of showing me your weapons?" Nidhan Singh asked.

"Come inside." Pitaji linked arms with Nidhan Singh and guided him through the door.

Dilbagh spoke, "Bhenji, can you come with me? I need to show you something."

I left the meal preparations to our mother and followed him. "What would you like to show me?" I couldn't see anything new from where I stood.

Dilbagh rubbed the palms of his hands together, and his back stiffened. "Actually . . . I wanted to ask how you like being married . . . because I do not know what to expect."

*Dilbagh is asking me for marital advice?*

"I am going to be honest with you, Veer. In the beginning, I did not think we had anything to share other than a will to honor our families. I am led by my emotions, and he follows his head. But our differences give what the other one needs."

"So, it is not a problem if we are different," Dilbagh spoke up, looking more relaxed.

"No, differences can be beneficial. What do you like about her?" Surely he had met her at least once, since she was a local girl.

"I have a feeling that she will let me be myself. I want someone who accepts me as I am, and I believe she will."

"Veer, you must accept her for who she is, too."

The morning of the wedding, we were seated in front of Harleen's familial home. I was wedged in between Mamiji and Jasmeet, resplendent in their matching peacock-blue salwar-kameez, their chunnis draped gracefully over their hair buns. Jasmeet had blossomed into a confident young woman, but her cheeks remained childlike in their chubbiness. She would be married soon.

"Oy hoy, happy to see you, Dhi." Mamiji gave me a tight hug. "Your salwar-kameez is soni."

I smiled at Mamiji.

My parents were in front of us, along with Chotu. In their tall and regal dastaars, my father and little brother exuded strength, while Mataji's silver hair shone like a crown in the sunlight.

Harleen wore a crimson silk salwar-kameez, its gold embroidery sparkling as she and Dilbagh circled the Holy Book. I closed my eyes in happiness, lost in the melody of prayer hymns. My bullheaded, patient, responsible veer was getting married.

Harleen was firmly gripping the cloth between them, looking anxious. *She is just like I was many seasons ago.*

Nidhan Singh was sitting next to Chotu. He leaned in close to my ear and whispered, "Remember us on our wedding day?"

"How can I forget?" I paused. "It feels good to see my family after so long. I know we can't make this journey often, so I am elated to be here. Are you enjoying yourself?"

"Yes. How could I not be? All of my favorite meals are being prepared specially for me." He grinned, knowing how I felt. "Why don't you make them for me at home?" He pinched my arm and laughed.

With the fourth and final lava phera, Dilbagh and Harleen were a married couple. Everyone rose to congratulate the bride and groom. Nidhan Singh joined my pitaji and veer and heartily patted Dilbagh's back.

I went to Harleen first. "Welcome to our family. I have a bhen now." She was trembling, and I gave her a hug.

Around us, the congratulatory chitter-chatter and laughter of wedding attendees sounded. Plates of laddoos and mitai of every shape were passed around, accompanied by the rich smell of ghee-soaked makki ki roti and saag.

I linked my arm in Harleen's and tugged her away from the crowd. "Harleen, I can imagine you are nervous. I felt the same way."

She lowered her shoulders, and her rail-straight back slumped. "You and your husband look so comfortable and at ease with one another." A dimple on her chin softened her sweet, heart-shaped face.

"It was difficult at first, but our love grew with time. Yours will, too. My brother is disciplined and lives by a strict code, but he will respect you. And he will protect you. And I promise, if you accept him, he will accept you as well."

Harleen's eyes lit up as she smiled. Clasping her hand in mine, I gently tugged my sister-in-law—nay, my sister—back to her guests.

# TWELVE

The monsoons made a spectacular entry, the cries of koels and pied-crested cuckoos heralding the onset of rain. Water-laden clouds rode the winds blowing across Punjab and drenched our crops, bringing summer to a fruitful end. Soon, autumn presided over our land.

We still had no children many seasons after our marriage. I worried that we may never.

The sun was dim in the cloudless sky above us as Nidhan Singh and I sparred. I positioned myself with my feet planted shoulder-width apart, a posture to tackle a larger opponent—exactly as Pitaji had taught me. Though I was strong, a male fighter would usually be bigger than me, which meant that I had to constantly account for their natural advantage. Our swords crossed, and the impact jolted my arm. He swung to my left, and I countered. I lunged toward his torso, and he blocked me deftly with his shield. I kicked toward his abdomen, and he ducked beneath the sweeping kick. We leaped apart and circled each other.

"Bhag Kaur, you would be a petrifying opponent in battle."

"Teri meri ikk jindri." You are my life. By then, these words had fallen from my lips many times. Yet, each time they tasted sweeter than before on my tongue. In this era of war, we were lucky to have one another. I cherished every moment we spent nurturing our love.

He swung his sword toward me, but the attack was less forceful, restrained almost.

"Why are you holding back? I saw you practice with our neighbor yesterday, and you weren't gentle with him."

"It wasn't on purpose. I didn't want to hurt you, and my protective instinct took over." He cleared his throat and shook his arms. "It won't happen again. Stand back and prepare yourself."

With that, he slashed at me, attempting to slice my arm. I blocked his advance with a swift movement of my shield. I advanced toward him, my trident-studded turban leading the way. Nidhan Singh took a large step back, teetering off-balance. Sensing an opportunity, I stuck a foot out, and he landed on his backside. I gleefully brought the tip of my kirpan to his neck.

"Jit gaye! This is what you get for underestimating me."

That evening, I was deep in meditation under a peepul tree when Nidhan Singh knelt beside me and laid his hand on my shoulder. He looked pale and anxious.

"I have terrible news. The emperor's army has laid siege to Anandpur Sahib. It is my dharam to fight alongside the Guru." Nidhan Singh looked resolute. "I must leave now, Bhag Kaur."

"If it is your dharam, then it is also mine. I am coming with you."

"No, I cannot ask you to go. You must stay here and protect our home."

"You said yourself that I would be a fearful opponent in battle. I am a skilled warrior, and as a warrior, isn't it my dharam to fight? What use is my training, then?"

"I can understand how you feel. But what kind of a husband would I be if I knowingly sent you into a death trap?" he pleaded, warring emotions crossing his face.

"And what kind of wife would I be to send my husband to die? I am so upset with you. I can't even look at you." Hot tears flooded my eyes.

Nidhan Singh placed his hands on my shoulders and pulled me toward him. "Do you think I want to leave you, not knowing if I will return? Your safety gives me the courage to face our enemies."

I resisted his embrace at first. But looking at his troubled face, my back caved, and I turned around to cling to him.

"Fight with courage, carrying your spirit and mine with you."

A group of men from our village arrived on horseback later that day. One of them beckoned my husband, straight-faced and aloof.

"Oy, Nidhan Singh, prepare your horse. We must hurry!"

Nidhan Singh tied a basket of provisions I'd packed to the horse's back. He strapped his kirpan across his chest, having already donned his smaller battle weapons. Ma and I stood side by side in silence. He avoided meeting my gaze in the presence of the other men, which only further upset me. Finally, upon mounting his steed, he looked at me with sad eyes.

"I will make you proud. Wait for me."

I stood there frozen until the sound of hooves pounding the ground faded. *Will I ever see my husband again?*

But I was still angry at being left behind. It was every trained warrior's duty to come to the Guru's aid. Why should one capable of bearing life not be called to defend lives?

Then, another thought entered my mind. I had not bled in almost two moon cycles. If I were with child, I should accept that my place was at home. Perhaps Nidhan Singh sensed this, which would explain his reluctance to attack me during practice.

My peace was short-lived. Two nights after my husband left, I was resting on the manji when the warm rush of blood between my thighs arrived—an unwelcome guest. A storm gathered inside me. Desperate for an outlet, I meditated under the cool shade of a banyan tree, focusing on Naam, the eternal name of Waheguru. *I belong on the battlefield.*

At dinnertime, I resentfully shaped roti pede. Ma noticed my expression and set down the vessel of daal she was carrying.

"Dhi, I can imagine how you must be feeling. But let me tell you a story about my son, and maybe it will help you understand him better. After his pitaji died, I would sleep outside most nights. One morning, I woke up and noticed a wasps' nest as large as my head hanging from the tree I was resting under. I screamed in fear, and my puttar came running to my side."

She took a deep breath and continued, "He looked unperturbed and said, 'Ma, if we were attacked at this very moment, that colony could be used as a weapon to swarm our enemies.' Dhi, that is how he views life. You married a man who sees a mighty kirpan in an ordinary wood stick. He only sees the good in any situation, and perhaps you should, too."

A tidal wave of guilt washed over me. Ma returned to cleaning the daal, and we spent the evening in quiet companionship.

My husband's prolonged absence became unbearable. My imagination ran wild with all the horrific ways he could be killed in battle. I tried to focus on my chores—cooking, cleaning, and tending to the crops—to distract my restless mind. When time allowed, I practiced mastering my weapons. I kept myself occupied from sunup to sundown, because if I thought about my husband too long, I felt like I couldn't breathe.

I dreaded nightfall. Without the distractions of work, fears invaded my thoughts like intruders in the night. *Was my husband alive? Was our beloved Guru safe? Was there enough to eat, or were the men going hungry?* I was crumbling like an old fort under attack, worries blowing up my defenses and leaving me open to endless pain.

As a child, I heard numerous legends of the great battles fought by our brave Sikh ancestors. Not one story mentioned the hardship faced by those waiting at home for their loved ones to return.

Ma and I finished cleaning the kitchen one night, and we were preparing to sleep when the quiet was shattered. Outside, our horses were snorting, neighing, and stomping the ground. I jumped out of the manji and grabbed my sword from the corner of the room.

"Bhag Kaur, what's going on?" Ma whispered, clearly afraid.

"Stay inside. I am going to check on the horses."

I tiptoed outside to discover two turbaned men attempting to untie our horses. Their faces were hidden behind dark cloth. Goose bumps pricked my arms. My heart drummed in my chest as I moved toward them, sword drawn.

"Leave my horses alone!"

"And who will stop us if we don't? We know no man is here. Go inside, or we will kill you!" The men had paid me such scant attention that they failed to notice my sword.

"Leave the horses alone." Calm, unafraid, menacing. This time, one of the men turned to face me. I held my kirpan— flawless steel—steady and level, just like Pitaji had taught me.

"Weapons do not belong in the hands of a woman," he throatily crooned, mocking me. A hateful grin split the man's lips as he charged. He made an ill-timed move for my weapon's hilt.

"What kind of Sikhs are you? You bring shame to the title, taking advantage of innocent people when you should be fighting alongside the Guru." My blade shivered as the brute tried to wrestle it from me, but I held tight.

His eyes widened for a moment, and he snickered at me. "We enjoy this much more. What do you think you'll do to me with this kirpan, woman? Kill me?"

The thief pulled harder. I yanked the sword back, and his hand slipped. Instinct took over. I leaned forward and plunged my blade into his chest. Hot blood sprayed across my face. His mouth froze mid-scream, and he collapsed to the ground. I stood rooted in shock. The attack was meant to protect, a way to make him back off . . .

"Chudail! You've killed him!" The second thief charged at me, livid. But he stopped short when it became clear that I'd attack again.

"Are you going to be next?" My temples throbbed, and my eyes narrowed. I readied myself to attack.

He attempted to knock me down with his heavy frame. I pivoted just as he came close, and he crashed to the ground. I poked the sharp tip of my sword into his neck, and a wet trickle of blood dripped down to his chest. "I'll kill you, too, if you don't leave at once." I jabbed harder to show him I meant it.

"Please, Bhenji," the terrified man pleaded, "let me go."

I spat in the dirt and withdrew my sword, stepping aside. He disappeared into the starless night, dragging his accomplice's body behind him. I presumed he didn't want the man to be identified.

I collapsed to the ground in a heap, gasping for air. Ma rushed outside.

"Dhi, what happened? Is this blood?" She tried to wipe my face clean with her chunni and hug me, but I felt numb to her touch.

"Two men . . . came to steal our horses . . . and I killed one of them. I stabbed him in the heart. His accomplice ran away, don't worry." I was barely able to get the words out. My arms trembled, and Ma held me tight. We sat in silence until my breathing slowed down.

Ma squeezed my hand. "You saved our lives."

"They were thieves. I don't know if they'd have harmed us." My body hung heavy, and a buzzing numbness pulsed through me. *I killed an unarmed man.*

"Would you rather have taken the chance? You did what had to be done." Ma ushered me inside.

I curled up on the manji, trying to understand what I had done. Pitaji's words rang in my ears. *The battlefield is your holy ground. The double-edged sword is your prayer. Combat is your service. And victory is your karma.* He'd have been proud of me. But was I proud of myself?

Unable to fall asleep, I lay numbed by fear. Overwhelmed with guilt. *I saved our horses, so I have nothing to feel guilty about.* An icy discomfort settled in my chest, stifling me. Was the killing in self-defense? Yes, I decided. It had been self-defense. No, it hadn't—the man wasn't carrying a weapon. But he threatened me . . . Then, yes, again. Exhausted by my oscillating emotions, I tried to force myself to sleep by breathing deeply. But the air stuck in my throat as if an icy wind had blown in and frozen it solid.

I wished for sunrise but knew the night would be long.

The next day a courier arrived from Jhabal Kalan with a letter for me.

> *My dearest Bhag Kaur,*
>
> *May this letter find you and your family hale and hearty. I miss you dearly. We all do, even dull Dilbagh. Just yesterday, I plucked the sweetest mango I had eaten in a while and wished you were here for me to pelt you with it. You must have heard about what happened at Anandpur Sahib. Dearest Bhenji, tomorrow before sunrise, I must set off for battle. Dilbagh's wife is with child, so he will not come with me at this time. Please do not worry—I carry with me Pitaji's strength, Mataji's commitment, Dilbagh's honor, and your bravery. If I die, I will enter the eternal home of Waheguru. But if I survive, I will come to you first. Either outcome is a supreme blessing, Bhenji. So, do not cry for me.*
>
> *Waheguru Ji Ka Khalsa. Waheguru Ji Ki Fateh.*
>
> *Yours always,*
> *Chotu*

I clutched the letter to my chest as tears fell and smeared the ink.

Forty nights after I received the letter from Chotu, my husband returned. Hearing the sound of horses galloping our way, I dropped the vegetables I was washing to rush outside. *My beloved was finally home.*

Nidhan Singh had lost weight. His once healthy face looked emaciated. Bags hung under his red eyes, his cheeks had hollowed, and his scraggly beard was in need of a wash. He dismounted his steed and collapsed in a pile. I ran to him, throwing my arms around him and wiping the dirt off his face with my clothing.

He wrapped a weak arm around me and spoke in a scruffy whisper, "We were under siege for many moons—it was unbearable. Food supplies were exhausted. We resorted to eating the bark from trees to survive." He paused and took a deep breath. "Our elephants and horses were dying of starvation. No amount of pleading with the Guru would convince him to surrender. We had no choice but to leave, Bhag Kaur."

"What?" My sympathy was abruptly extinguished, like a fire doused with a pail of water. "You abandoned our Guru?"

"We did what we had to do, my love. I wish you could understand."

"It was your dharam as a warrior to stay with the Guru." The words were trapped in my throat, and I struggled to breathe. "You should not have prevented me from going. Left behind, I was forced to kill a man to save our horses. I did what I had to; I followed my dharam."

"It must have been hard for you, too." He reached for my hand, but I pushed him away.

"Bhag Kaur . . . I have to tell you something."

A sick feeling came over me as Nidhan Singh opened and closed his mouth a few times in hesitation. I was not going to like what he had to say. His eyes were barely open, but tears started to form.

"Chotu . . . is no more. He was given an honorable cremation, and he is with Waheguru. I am so sorry—"

I raised my hand abruptly to stop him from talking. My Chotu. Gone. "My veer died with honor, but you scurried away like a rabbit running from a fox?" I couldn't control my cruel words.

By then, his mother had joined us and wrapped her arms around her puttar. Her eyes warned me to stop, but I didn't pay her heed.

"If I had been there, I would have saved my brother's life!"

I grabbed my kirpan and disappeared into the fields. Deep inside the ocean-green fields, I pulled the blade from the protection of its sheath and swung at the jute plants surrounding me. The weak plants fell to the ground like the ashes of the dead. Like the ashes of Chotu.

I swung until my arms stung with pain. *My cowardly husband. My dead veer.* I swung until sweat pooled on my skin and felt nothing but weariness in my arms. I swung until I nearly collapsed.

When I returned home, Nidhan Singh was resting on a manji inside. He looked peaceful. Angry as I was, he was my husband, battle-weary and almost drained of life.

Ma was leaning over the chulha to start a fire. I sat next to her and dutifully helped prepare a meal.

I hastily set a plate of food down beside him, unable to look at him. "Here, eat."

He tried to hold my hand, his eyes soft with pity. "You must be hurting terribly."

I gently pulled my hand away and left his side.

# THIRTEEN

It had been many days since Nidhan Singh's return.

I escaped to the stream behind the house to be alone while my husband tended to the farm. The gentle sounds of flowing water felt like a balm for my troubled soul. The earthy scent of moss filled my nostrils. I ran my fingers through the air, reaching for colors that grew brighter with each passing moment. A jackdaw hopped around on the dewy grass, looking for its morning meal. Something in the way it moved—a lightness—struck me with wonder.

A picture of Chotu laughing flashed before my eyes. After losing my mamaji and Gurdas, I tried to push the sadness into a far corner of my heart. I thought I had learned to conquer those feelings, to be ready for the next time my heart would shatter. I was wrong. You don't build immunity to grief.

For the first time since my veer's death, I cried. I never asked how my veer died. In fact, I never spoke about him with my husband again. I had become my mother, suppressing my emotions, not allowing anyone else to feel the discomfort of my sadness. Grief and confusion, guilt and anger, and love, above all, poured from within. *Push it all out.* I let out a guttural cry that echoed in my heart, if not the world. I couldn't distinguish between the two, and it didn't matter.

Crimson bougainvillea flowers floated downstream like blood in the water. I sank into the muddy earth, wrapping my arms around myself, and rocked back and forth, trying to soothe my heart. Chotu's death had ripped out a part of me, one full of love. Memories of our childhood came rushing back—the wrestling matches, the long afternoons spent plucking mangoes, his good-natured teasing. I remembered the look of love in Chotu's eyes at my wedding. My parents were devastated that Chotu never married.

I felt a numbness creeping over me. Was it shock? No, it felt as though my broken heart was donning steel armor. It cut through my depression and dried my tears. It made me feel powerful, indestructible. Nothing and no one could hurt me now. My heart had been broken for the last time. I breathed deeply, allowing the feeling to sink in, taking control of it before it controlled me.

The crunching of fallen leaves brought me back to the present.

"Bhag Kaur? Are you well?" Nidhan Singh took in my puffy face.

"I will be . . ."

He wrapped his arm around me and rubbed my back. "You're trembling."

The hush was broken by the droning of bees. Nidhan Singh opened up to me. "On guard duty, I would listen to the other men talk. We are not alone in our struggles. Wars are being waged in many other faraway lands; disputes over taxes and borders are common. They, too, fight to the death like us."

"It seems as though war is the way of our world." I squeezed his hand gently.

"I will never forget what I witnessed at Anandpur Sahib. I've never seen so much blood. Severed limbs and lopped-off heads littered the fields. The screams of dying men still echo in my mind. On the battlefield, a warrior salivates for the kill, another's skull cracks, and a knife rasps bone. War can make a sane man go mad; a kind one turn bloodthirsty. And hunger makes you do things you would not dream of doing. There was so little food—we made do on one fruit a day or half a roti. When we ran out, our men were eating tree bark." He inhaled deeply.

"But I would do it again. You know this." He faced me, commanding our eyes to meet. "Because this is what I remember. This is what keeps me strong—you and me. When I think of us, I want to recall this moment, surrounded by the beauty of our land. My sweetest memories are with you. I want to die with them staying sweet, untouched by the bitterness of time." Nidhan Singh clasped my hand. "Know this, Bhag Kaur. In this lifetime—and in the ones to follow—you will always be my greatest love." He pressed his lips against mine, their salty taste so familiar to me.

A sudden, unexpected relief washed over me. Nidhan Singh—my beloved husband—was by my side, safe. "I am sorry for being angry at you for so long. You survived an unimaginable ordeal . . ." I trailed off, knowing my brother didn't.

"Chotu was braver than I could ever have been. I think of him every day, even if I don't talk about him."

The beauty of my husband's love. I reached out to dry his tears. "I forgive you. You, too, were brave. And you will always be my one love."

Winter arrived, an icy serenade. Silvery-brown leaves had fallen proudly on the frozen ground and lay bejeweled with frost that crunched underfoot.

A messenger from the Khalsa army arrived in Patti. With a matted beard and dirt-crusted hair, the sunken-cheeked man looked like many who returned from the war front. The residents of our village gathered around him, eager for news.

"Aurangzeb's soldiers, aided by the armies of the hill rajas, surrounded Anandpur Sahib for many moons. The town ran out of food, and our people were dying of hunger. The emperor's generals agreed to a ceasefire, promising Sikhs safe passage if they abandoned Anandpur Sahib. Our Guru hesitated, but he finally agreed and left the town accompanied by his family and a small band of loyal men." The man brushed a stray hair from his beard before continuing, "He did not leave the town unguarded. Bibi Dalair Kaur Ji, a trusted Sikh, remained. A small band of Sikhs aided her, most of them women, to keep the enemy at bay."

"Bibi? A woman protecting the Anandgarh fort?" I looked at Nidhan Singh. He lowered his eyes.

"Soon after the Guru left, enemy soldiers stormed the fort. Our people were betrayed by a deceitful promise the emperor's generals never meant to keep. Bibi Dalair Kaur scrambled to prepare for battle while the enemy looted the town and set fire to what remained. Surrounded by a blazing inferno, she ordered her sisters to pick up their weapons. They had received amrit, and they were ready to die fighting for their freedom." The messenger punched the air with his fist.

"Our adversaries assumed the fort was empty, and they were caught off guard by a rain of bullets that killed many of their men. They broke their ranks and ran for their lives. Their leader then commanded his troops to fire a cannon, reducing one of the walls of the fort to a pile of rubble." The messenger paused and allowed us a moment to process the news.

"Those cowards attacked when our backs were turned," a birdlike woman spoke up and turned to look at me. "I've seen you maneuver a sword, Bhag Kaur. You could fight our enemies, like Bibi Dalair Kaur Ji."

A woman in a red salwar-kameez elbowed her. "What is this nonsense you're saying to her?"

I focused my gaze on the first woman, stroking the strap that held my sheathed blade.

"I should." The words felt like shards of ice on my tongue.

The messenger raised his head and cleared his throat, drawing us back to his narration. "Eventually, the Khalsa women ran out of bullets, and their capture was imminent. Bibi Dalair Kaur proclaimed that the time had come to die with honor. Their adversaries were closing in, so there was no time to waste. They positioned themselves behind the damaged wall, the only point of entry, and waited to pounce on the soldiers. When our enemies saw the armed women, they paused in confusion—they had never encountered a battalion of female warriors before.

"Their leader shouted, 'Cowards, are you afraid of women? They are gifts for you—capture them and do what you want with your reward.' In response, Bibi Dalair Kaur said without fear, 'We are the hunters, not the hunted. Come and find out for yourself!'"

Another from our village interjected, "Did she really say that?"

"She did. I heard it myself as I was there, fighting alongside her. A fierce battle commenced, and we lost many brave Kaurs and Singhs. Then the invaders fired the cannon again, and much of the fort's ramparts collapsed, burying our fighters in the rubble. These brave Sikhs' bodies may have perished, but their souls attained the highest honor that day. The attackers did not kill everyone—a handful of Kaurs escaped, as did I. We are traveling great distances to inform others of what happened." The man lowered his head.

"Waheguru Ji, may the fallen receive salvation," said a yellow-turbaned man, closing his eyes and pressing his hands together.

I felt like I was on fire. Innocent women were killed in a cowardly attack. *When will this end?* We deserved to live in peace, without constantly having to defend our people against aggression and treachery. The only bright light in this tragedy was the shining example of Bibi Dalair Kaur Ji. I admired her courage.

My thoughts were interrupted by the Khalsa emissary, who looked like he was about to say something. *There is more?* He asked the women and children to return home before he spoke again. Though puzzled by his request, many complied. But not me. Nidhan Singh squeezed my hand. In this time of uncertainty, I was grateful that we still had each other. I accepted his strength as my own.

"In the meanwhile, the Guru and his entourage were traveling south when they were pursued by the enemy; their promises for safe passage were revealed to be lies. Guru Gobind Singh Ji and his warriors resisted courageously, but his two youngest sons, as well as his mataji, were betrayed by an old servant, who turned them over to Emperor Aurangzeb's general in Sirhind."

"Shame on this man. He is a disgrace to our people!" a shout rose from the crowd, and everyone nodded in agreement.

"In Sirhind, the boys were offered sanctuary if they renounced Sikhism. Both of them refused. The two young puttar were immured, and upon hearing the news, their grandmother passed away." As the words left the messenger's mouth, a cold gust of wind knocked us back.

"Oy hoy!" A silver-haired woman threw herself to the ground and wailed in agony.

I gasped in horror and lost my balance for a moment. How could someone do this to children? The Guru's sons, no more than eight years old, were entombed in a brick wall until they suffocated to death. *I'll avenge the Guru!*

The Sikh from Anandpur Sahib tugged at his scraggly beard, struggling to form his next words. "The Guru, unaware of their tragic deaths, trudged onward. He was forced to defend himself at Chamkaur, where he was ambushed. His two older sons died in the skirmish."

"How could this have happened? Our Guru lost all four of his bachche within a matter of days!" I stomped my foot hard, wishing I could crush these cruel men like ants.

"Only the Guru and a handful of Sikhs survived the ambush at Chamkaur. They changed direction to avoid capture—their escape aided by the Guru's Muslim allies—and hid in the forests of Machhiwara."

A soft-spoken woman piped up, "Can you imagine our divine Guru scrounging for wild berries while mourning the death of his sons? I shudder to think of the immense pain he must have suffered."

"Indeed, he suffered terribly," the messenger agreed. "But pain can bring forth weeds or blossom into the most beautiful flowers. He was reunited with a band of loyal Sikhs at Jatpura, where he learned of the tragic deaths of his younger sons and his beloved mother. Channeling his unfathomable grief, he composed a letter in Persian addressed to Emperor Aurangzeb. This letter, the Zafarnama, was an indictment of the emperor and his commanders for breaking their oath to guarantee safe passage to Sikhs leaving Anandpur Sahib. Two Sikhs were dispatched to deliver this letter to the emperor."

I recalled the warmth and strength that radiated from our Guru on that distant Baisakhi day. And now, I tried to picture him in this moment of immeasurable sorrow—his brilliant eyes widening before closing under the weight of grief and anger, his mighty hands clasped in fists, his body standing tall, ready for the next attack upon his soul—and I felt my rage coming to a boil.

Nidhan Singh looked distraught. "I cannot believe I abandoned the Guru during this terrible time."

"Finding the pursuing host close upon his heels, our Guru has decided to face them in battle. He has set up camp in Khidrana and is rallying his forces. This concludes my message to the Khalsa."

The Sikh from Anandpur Sahib was determined to spread the news as far and wide as he could, and shortly after replenishing his provisions, he left. His horse disappeared into a cloud of dust.

This brave warrior on a mission had given me mine, and I accepted it with dignity.

# FOURTEEN

"Bhag Kaur." We had retired for the night, Nidhan Singh lying in the manji next to mine. "Why have you been icy with me?"

"Must I say it?" I rubbed my hands together for warmth. Moonlight flooded our room through a small window.

"I shouldn't have left the Guru. I know this, and yet, you continue to remind me."

"Our Guru needs warriors right now." I rolled on my side, turning my back to him.

"You did hear the messenger say that most of the women defending Anandpur Sahib died, didn't you? I suppose you'd prefer that fate." Nidhan Singh rose. "I'll sleep outside. Your parents and veer should be here tomorrow to visit."

"It is cold outside. Please stay inside."

"Teinu ki," he mumbled.

My brother, accompanied by Mataji and Pitaji, arrived at midday. My mother-in-law was visiting her dhi in Amritsar, so it had only been Nidhan Singh and me at home. Dilbagh now had a young son, Harinder, and Harleen remained with her parents to care for him. From the stories my parents told me, Harinder Singh was an energetic child, all smiles and giggles, his arms and legs still chubby with rolls of baby fat. *Will I have a bachcha of my own someday?*

Mataji was helping me make roti outside, gushing over her grandson. "Whenever Harinder sees me, he comes running to me, demanding that I make him hot parate."

"He resembles Dilbagh, but his nature is like our Chotu." Pitaji looked away.

A painful silence followed as he sorted crops with Nidhan Singh and Dilbagh. My father refused to speak of my little brother's death. He died honorably—there was nothing to add.

"A messenger delivered the tragic news that the Guru's four sons and mother were killed. Our Guru is fleeing capture, and we must help him."

"We, too, were informed." Dilbagh's voice dipped with sorrow. "I plan to join him at Khidrana." He looked at Nidhan Singh for support.

Nidhan Singh set down the basket of vegetables he was carrying. "Bhag Kaur, there is something you must know. I didn't find the courage to tell you this before, but I can no longer keep it a secret. During the long siege at Anandpur Sahib, men were starving. Many were on the verge of death. Having lost all hope of victory, forty of us went to the Guru and pleaded with him to surrender. He refused to discuss the idea, and we chose to leave. You have to understand, we wanted to see our families—I wanted to see you. However, Guru Gobind Singh Ji was dismayed by our lack of faith. He made us sign a document stating that we were abandoning our dharam and that we were no longer his Sikhs . . . And I did." He hung his head in shame.

Fury wrapped me in an all-controlling expanse; my patience burned to a crisp in the wildfire that raged within me. Nothing and no one would contain me any longer. I would not allow them to. *It has been within me to take hold of my power as a woman.*

"Guru Gobind Singh Ji declined to negotiate with the emperor, and you abandoned him? How could you do that? You deserted him when he needed you the most. Where is your courage? Where is your faith? The Guru is right—you are not a true Sikh.

"Nidhan Singh, if we do not stand up for our beliefs, we are lost. Our Guru sacrificed everything—even his family—for his people. As his followers, we may die on the battlefield. This is true. But we will all die one day anyway, and how fortunate would we be to die fighting by his side? Don't you understand that?

"If you won't fight, then I will! I will join him in Khidrana. You can take care of the home. You can take my churra and wear them! If you want to regain honor, come with me now, unrestrained by the fear of death."

Nidhan Singh's bloodshot eyes met my fiery gaze. "You haven't been on the battlefield. You haven't nearly starved to death defending a man who sees no reason. We have lost the war against the emperor, and the Guru will not admit defeat. You play with your weapons at home, but you cannot imagine the devastation thrust upon our people by this war. I have given everything. I still desire victory, but it is unattainable. I neither want Sikhs to continue to suffer nor do I want all of them dead!"

I tried to gather myself, but I was shattered by his words. My parents and brother walked away to avoid interfering in our argument.

Nidhan Singh took a deep breath. "I can't believe you shamed me in front of your parents."

Guilt washed over me. I wrapped my arms around him and pressed my face to his chest, holding on until he released the tension in his back. "That was unfair. Please forgive me."

"Despite what you may think of my character now, I will not watch my wife ride into battle while I stay home. We will face death together on the battlefield. You have my word, Bhag Kaur."

Nidhan Singh, Dilbagh, and I donned our Khalsa Swarupa, battle armor. I secured my royal-blue robe with a cloth tied around my waist and covered my long hair with a saffron turban. The three of us strapped our larger weapons and tucked smaller ones into our clothing.

Outside, winter's winds nipped at our fingers and toes. My parents watched us in silence. Finally, Pitaji couldn't contain himself any longer. "You three are very dear to me. We have already lost Chotu. I don't think I can bear it if anything were to happen to you."

"I cannot lose all of you." There was no anger on my mother's face, only resignation. I saw myself through her eyes. She hadn't been restraining me since I was young—she was protecting me, cocooning me in her love. My mataji had always known who I was. And now, her greatest fear clasped her in its grip—the thought that I might die.

Dilbagh and I hugged my parents, knowing it might be the last time we saw them. Tears welled in my mother's eyes as I struggled to release myself from her tight hold.

"Mataji, you are stronger than you think. Did you think we learned to be brave from Pitaji alone?" We mounted our steeds, provisions loaded, and set off.

We rode from village to village, rounding up the men who had deserted the Guru at Anandpur Sahib. I urged them to ride with us to Khidrana to regain their honor.

"This woman is Bhag Kaur, Dhi of Malo Shah. He himself has trained her to fight! There can be no better leader to ride off into battle with," one of the wives shouted. It was the woman who had shushed my supporter in the presence of the messenger from Anandpur Sahib. *Oy, the irony!*

The men nodded in respect. One of them spoke up, "I have seen her practice, and she is a strong fighter. Her skills with the kirpan are impressive. She has even defeated her husband in swordplay."

Embarrassment flashed across Nidhan Singh's face, and he looked away.

A man in a blue turban stepped forward. "Bhag Kaur Ji, I am Mahan Singh. Every day, I feel a knife stabbing my heart. Those of us who deserted the Guru burn with guilt. How can we face him and ask for his forgiveness after what we did?"

His words invigorated me. "It isn't too late to redeem yourselves. Answer his call for support now, and he will forgive your misdeed."

The crowd erupted in cheers. All forty warriors, Nidhan Singh included, vowed to return to the Guru to reclaim their honor as Sikhs. Resplendent in the Khalsa Swarupa, I led the men in the direction of the Guru's encampment.

Our progress was slow and painful. Our route went through snow-covered terrain, dense with trees and shrubbery. On the first night, we used our swords like machetes to clear through treacherously icy foliage in the dark.

I was afraid of attracting attention if we continued to trample through the forest like a herd of elephants. "If we march together like this, we risk capture. Instead, we should travel in small groups using unfrequented paths. We will be faster that way." The men agreed, and we split up into units of ten.

The journey was arduous, and the cold enervating. Some of my group swayed in exhaustion, almost falling off their horses. Despite my own fatigue, I pushed forward, encouraging the men to keep up when they lagged. The thick overcoats of buffalo hide provided little warmth. Our teeth chattered, and the cold left our fingers stiff and frigid. My breath was fire that set my lungs aflame.

"Bhenji, I will lead us to battle," Dilbagh proclaimed, riding up to join me.

"Nonsense. You can hardly keep your eyes open. Every so often, you close them until a vigorous breeze rouses you." An icy breeze sent shivers up my spine.

My veer scoffed at me and attempted to gain the lead by pushing his tired horse harder. "Oy, faster!"

Nidhan Singh hadn't said much of anything since we'd left.

"Are you well?" I asked.

"Some of the men look at me in amusement because my wife is leading me to the front." He glanced at me.

"Halt!"

Our group skidded to a stop. "There isn't a man here who did not run away from the battlefield. And every single one of you is here because your wife or sister urged you to return to the Guru. Remember that!"

All the men lowered their heads in shame, except for my husband, who raised his high and looked straight ahead. Satisfied, I turned and prodded my horse to pick up the pace.

In the mornings, we tried to sleep in well-hidden areas, but we struggled to relax our weary bodies on the frozen ground. We were supplementing our meals with tree bark because the provisions we carried ran low. Hunger and thirst were our constant companions, but our faith sustained us.

"Tonight is the final leg of our journey. We should be with

the Guru by sunrise." I strapped my belongings to my horse, preparing to mount him, when I noticed that one of the young men had lacerated his knee. I tore off a piece of my clothing and wrapped the cloth around his wound.

The young Sikh, Prahlad Singh, looked at me and said, "You remind me of my mataji. Like her, you wrap the binding so it doesn't come free." He couldn't have been any older than Gurdas when he left.

I pointed to my brother and smiled. "I bandaged many of Dilbagh's childhood injuries, so I have had practice."

Prahlad Singh looked lost in thought. "My mataji stopped eating after my veer died. No amount of begging worked. A dark cloud obscured her once-bright personality; I tried to be the person that made her happy, but it didn't work. She didn't want to live for me. And then, one day, she stopped drinking water, and I watched her body wither into nothingness. I didn't realize you could die from sadness."

I tucked the end of the bandage and hugged the young man. "You are my puttar. We are the children of Waheguru, making us one family."

"Thank you, Mata Bhag Kaur," the young warrior replied.

Guru Gobind Singh Ji had set up camp in the semi-arid lands around Khidrana. I attempted to smooth out my matted hair and rub the dirt off my face before we entered the enclosure, when I remembered why I was there. I squashed any concerns of meeting him looking less-than-presentable. I guided my horse uphill, prodigal battalion in tow.

Makeshift shelters had been set up on top of a hill. A small herd of horses was tethered to the bare-branched trees close by. An impressive arsenal was on display, glinting in the cold sunlight. Each weapon was gracefully wrought and covered in obsessive detail, from hilt to intricately etched blade. A bitterly cold, dry wind blew over the encampment and coated everything in a thin layer of snow.

Gaunt-looking Sikhs surrounded the Guru, their faces streaked with mud. It had been six winters since I had laid eyes on our Guru. Though he looked older—grief had aged him—his radiant presence still commanded attention. We approached him and lowered our heads in respect.

I bowed and touched his feet. "Guru Ji, I am Bhag Kaur, Dhi of Malo Shah and great-niece of Bhai Langah. I have brought these warriors back to you. We vow to never again abandon you. We vow to fight with honor."

He lifted me by my shoulders and hugged me, speaking with great tenderness. "You come from a family of devoted Sikhs. Your great-uncle dedicated his life to my dadaji, Guru Hargobind Singh Ji. I treasure your presence here." His words filled me with peace and my fatigue melted away.

He turned to the men behind me. "I forgive you, my puttar. Waheguru's love is immeasurable, as is mine. Chaupa Singh, ready them for battle. I must pray now." The Guru retreated into a nearby tent.

A thick-limbed man with a mud-caked beard stepped forward. "Nawab Wazir Khan's army approaches us from the east. A cavalry of a few thousand men should be here by sunrise tomorrow."

With this grave announcement, the air grew thick with tension. Anxiety bubbled up in my chest. *Push away the fear.* Dilbagh closed his eyes in silent prayer while my husband clenched and unclenched his fists at his sides.

"We are in desert terrain, so many of them will be weak from thirst. How can we use the lack of water to our advantage?" Nidhan Singh spoke up, ever the calm voice of reason.

Chaupa Singh nodded. "Good question. Thirst can drive even battle-hardened soldiers insane. There is a dry well at the bottom of this hill. We'll station ourselves there."

My pitaji's lessons came back to me. *The most important skill you will learn is deception. The blows your enemy doesn't see coming do the most damage.*

"We will pretend to guard the well. Our adversaries have no way of knowing that it is dry, and they will try to capture it. We can keep them occupied while we plan a counter-attack from another direction."

"Correct, Bhag Kaur Ji," said Chaupa Singh, turning to the assembly. "Are you all prepared?"

We nodded. A fierce wind whipped the tent, a harbinger of what was to come.

"No one ever feels completely ready for battle, but you try to be prepared. Ensure that you each have armor, weapons, and a well-rested horse. It takes strength to remain steadfast in your faith. The moment you are compelled to use the sword in hatred, let the weapon clatter to the ground. You are Sikhs, warriors who possess the inner strength and self-control to follow their principles in the face of intolerance and oppression.

My brother was dismembered by the enemy. I pieced his body together to cremate him." Chaupa Singh rubbed his eyes with his left hand; his thumb and index finger had been reduced to nubs.

He noticed our eyes follow his hand. "This is nothing. I was trying to save my brother, and my fingers were slashed. Unlike me, our dear Guru never complains of his unimaginable suffering. Instead, he focuses on worship." Tears formed at the corners of his eyes. "But there is no place for mourning and grief on the battlefield. Our hearts are strong. Our eyes are clear."

I lowered my head in respect.

Chaupa Singh led us toward the throng of warriors huddled around a campfire. Smoke laced with the odor of horse dung filled my nostrils. In front of us, men were balancing swords between their teeth. Two blue-turbaned Sikhs practiced their swordplay in a mock battle while another group of men shot arrows at a makeshift target marked with ash on a tree trunk.

"Ja!" one of them shouted triumphantly as an arrow hit the target dead-on.

Planks of wood had been placed in a circle, an arm's length apart. A long-legged warrior carrying two heavy clay pots tied to a pole jumped from plank to plank to improve his balance and strength.

"Look at their discipline. Knowing that they face an almost certain death at daybreak tomorrow, they still train with such fervor," I said. Nidhan Singh nodded knowingly.

"You should ready your swords." Chaupa Singh pointed to

a weary-eyed man seated by the fire. We held our blades above the fire and, once they were malleable, sharpened them with a rough stone.

"Come, let us practice." Swords sheathed, Chaupa Singh guided our group to an open area.

The long-legged warrior had left his training station and limped past us. "We may meet our maker, Veer. We are sorely outnumbered."

Prahlad Singh shuddered at his words, his eyes wide. I patted his back reassuringly, but inside, fear thickened like sugarcane juice boiling. *We are going to sacrifice our lives.*

In the open area, wooden practice weapons lay scattered on the ground. We separated into four groups, nodding to indicate that we were ready.

Leaping forward, I went low, aiming for Prahlad Singh's legs. He jumped up in perfect time, stepped back, and flipped his sword to his right hand. He lunged, taking a sideways sweep at my midriff. His sword crossed mine as I blocked the strike.

"Each group must advance on each other without warning. An attack may come from any side, and we must always be prepared for multiple opponents," Chaupa Singh bellowed.

Dilbagh Singh stepped into my view, and I leaped at him. Seeing me from the corner of his eye, he spun around and blocked my forward slash. Nidhan Singh swept into the chaos, and our wooden swords met. I aimed my stick at his knees to disrupt his balance. He steadied himself and retaliated with a jab at my throat. I jumped back to retreat. I was absorbed in the intensity, my body a blur of action.

We practiced until dusk. After a sparse meal, we gathered to pray. And in this way, we were prepared—body, mind, and soul—to meet the Mughal army at daybreak.

# FIFTEEN

"We will rise early, so get enough rest," Chaupa Singh commanded. "I will remain on guard duty throughout the night."

I couldn't sleep, even in the comfort of Nidhan Singh's strong arms. Stiff from the cold, I got up just before sunrise and stretched my limbs. We donned the blue-and-orange Khalsa Swarupa in silence, helping each other for what might be the last time.

We knelt before our Guru as he led us in a battle prayer calling upon Waheguru, our eternal protector, to be our shield. With this invocation, we picked up our mighty weapons.

We were ready.

It was time to take our positions. Guru Gobind Singh Ji and his band of loyal Sikhs stationed themselves uphill. I led the battalion of forty warriors downhill to guard the dry well.

"We will fight here," I commanded. "We are strong. We will have no fear. As Sikh warriors, we are ready to fight for justice. Waheguru Ji Ka Khalsa! Waheguru Ji Ki Fateh!"

Forty brave men cheered, "We are ready. We have no fear of death. Waheguru Ji Ka Khalsa! Waheguru Ji Ki Fateh!"

Knowing we were severely outnumbered, we planned an ambush. We created a phantom camp of tents by draping sheets across tall bushes. Then my men hid in the greenery nearby, ready to pounce when the enemy soldiers attacked the empty tents.

We stood steadfast and strong, waiting for the Mughals. My eyes roved the desert landscape to seek out hidden threats, a habit born from my training. Then I spotted a sea of turbaned heads on the horizon. Where did one soldier's turban end and the next one begin?

With the sun rising behind them, it looked as though they had stepped off the giant ball of fire and onto the battleground. Dressed in imperial red and green, the men marched in tight formation, like the carefully woven thread of a blanket. Metal armor encased their bodies, glinting in the early light. Their heavy footfalls thundered, creating a sandstorm at their feet. As they came closer, I could see matted hair peeking through their turbans. Teeth bared, their mouths salivated at the sight of the well. They were thirsty, as Nidhan Singh predicted.

Beads of sweat sprouted from my forehead. I prayed for strength, my heart thick with dread. How had sweet-natured Chotu endured this? How did he feign courage in the face of death? My hands trembled, and the bow I held vibrated. *Push through the fear. Remember why you are here!* My heart blazed with an inner fire. With a straight face, pursed lips, and furrowed brow, the mighty scream heard at my birth echoed inside me.

The Guru's men fired arrows downhill, catching the enemy soldiers by surprise. The whizzing arrows rained death. Men fell, their faces frozen in shock. The ones left standing seethed at being caught unaware, and they bolted toward the deceptive tent bushes. At that, my men and I leaped out from our hiding places, charging like lions.

A blue-and-orange body fell to the ground on my left. One of our men. Who was it? Before I could look, a hefty soldier charged at me. My hand instinctively moved to my bow, steady at my side, a part of me. I slid an arrow out of my quiver and nocked it, clasping the rawhide grip of the bow. I couldn't tell where my arm ended and the bow began. *Pull and release.* The arrow flew straight, right on target. My first kill.

I knelt by his body and said a short prayer. *May I lay down this weapon when there is peace in our land. And then my heart will be my only weapon.*

A cacophony of battle cries punctuated by screams of pain filled the air. Swords clashed; arrows and spears flew. Bodies dropped around me, bloodied and lifeless. My mind went numb. Spears stood straight and tall, their tips embedded in the hearts of men on the ground. Friend or foe? They all looked alike in death. Green-and-red uniforms overpowered the battlefield. *Mataji and Pitaji will lose all their bachche today.*

Sweat soaked my clothes, though it was the dead of winter. My neighbor's spear was knocked out of his hands. His opponent stabbed him in the heart and then yanked his blood-soaked sword out. My neighbor stumbled to his death.

"Ahhhhh!" I clutched my stomach and retched up a thin stream of vomit.

The soldier turned his attention to me. He was slender, frail even, not what I expected a warrior to look like. He snarled at me. I shook off my nausea and met his gaze, reaching into my quiver.

"You will die for killing my comrade." I nocked an arrow and released it just as he charged at me, sword in hand. The arrow found its mark, and his eyes widened in surprise. He tumbled backward as he unsuccessfully attempted to pull it out of his chest.

I scanned the battlefield for Dilbagh and Nidhan Singh. *Where are they? Are they alive?* Bodies lay thick over the wintry ground, a garish scarlet staining the frosted white. Warrior after warrior attacked me—I exhausted my arrows.

A strong-armed warrior thrust his sword forward to attack me head-on. I positioned myself as Pitaji taught me and leaped to one side as he neared, shield ready to fend off his charge. He gasped when he realized I was a woman, reacting just long enough for me to make my move. With one powerful jab from my steel-tipped spear, my attacker lurched and collapsed to the ground.

Before I could draw my breath, the sound of heavy footsteps pounded the ground behind me. I dropped the spear and whipped out my sword. I whisked around and lashed out at my attacker. Our swords clashed. I charged at him, and he lost his footing. He fell to the ground, throat exposed. Open for the kill.

The hairs on my neck rose instinctually. Another warrior charged at me on his steed, and I raised my blood-soaked sword in front of my face. The hatchet-faced man jumped off his horse and sprinted toward me, his spear aimed at my heart. His long weapon proved to be a disadvantage. He neared, and I jumped aside and stabbed him. He fell to his death as I slid my kirpan out from inside him.

I launched myself at two warriors with a thrust and parry. Fear unsteadied their footing; I slashed the leg of one and sliced an ear off the other. Horse hooves galloped toward me, and I positioned myself to shield my body. An ox-size soldier bounded in my direction, his eyes glowering with rage. I sized him up, noting our similar heights but vastly dissimilar body weights. His gaze made my palms sweat. *The battlefield is your holy ground. The double-edged sword is your prayer. Combat is your service. And victory is your karma.* I lunged toward him with my sword drawn, and our weapons clashed.

"Ahhh! I will tear you apart!" His scream boomed like the monsoon skies. Dagger in his hand, he sprinted toward me, underestimating his opponent's skill. I launched into a perfect kick and knocked him down. He dropped the dagger. I scooped it up and stabbed him in the heart. I suppose you could say his weapon fulfilled its duty, even if it did not bring about the death he'd hoped for. The same fury-loaded eyes now looked up at me, motionless. A slight chill rushed through my body, and I shuddered.

Over and again, I defended myself. How many men had I killed? With each passing moment, our army grew smaller. How long could forty men stave off a countless horde?

"Who are you?" A dagger-sharp, dagger-cold voice mocked me from behind. "A woman? Where are your cowardly men?

No, I know. We've killed them all. You miss your pitaji? Or your veere? Worse—your husband?"

My veins scalded. I whisked around to face the hurler of the condescending words. He sought to distract me with anger. How stupid did he think I was? There was no dignified reply, and in any case, how did you reply to one with no dignity? The man carelessly awaited an answer instead of attacking me. He stood at least a head taller than me, with a lean build and narrow shoulders. He'd lost his shield but held a sword in his left hand. His weapon appeared shiny and sharp—a new sword. I presumed him to be well-trained, but the longer you handled a particular weapon, the more skilled you became at maneuvering it. He couldn't have perfected the use of this brand-new blade. A part of his armor covering his torso was missing. His crooked-toothed smile and haughty demeanor annoyed me. I'd enjoy taking him down.

"There is water in that well over there," I said, gesturing to the east. "Aren't you thirsty for some refreshment?" As I hoped, my offhand comment caught him by surprise, and he looked toward the well. I scooped up my spear and held it behind my back. He didn't notice.

"I am thirsty. Let me rid myself of you, and then I can drink all the water I want," he snarled.

With that, the long-legged soldier charged at me, arrogance obscuring him to the danger that lay ahead. I took my stance, whisking my spear from behind and holding it perpendicular to my stomach. He ran right into it. Our eyes met upon impact, his face contorted in disbelief before his body collapsed. The force of the attack jolted me and splintered my spear in two. I gasped, but I couldn't stop now. We came willing to lose everything for our cause. I had already lost my swords and now my spear. Pitaji's training raced to my mind like an ocean wave crashing ashore. *In times of war, you reserve your worn arms until you've lost all the weapons you hold.* The next moment, my hip-pocket dagger sailed into a man's neck. My turban's trident stabbed another. I used my chakrams one by one, killing or maiming my attackers. Not a single weapon of mine went unused.

Swords ground as bodies fell. The lurid, devastating scene fell over my eyes like a ghastly nightmare. There were severed heads, disfigured bodies, torsos twisted in unnatural ways, bloodshot eyes, and gaping mouths. Horses whinnied and neighed. My head spun. *We were not fighting to prevail; we were fighting to survive. We sought freedom to practice our way of life.*

And then, far to my right, a gargantuan man clambered up the hill toward my husband. Nidhan Singh charged instinctually at the colossus, but he held only a dagger. He'd never survive an attack by the sword-wielding assailant.

"NOOOOOO!" I ran toward my husband, begging my feet to move faster.

But it was too late. The overfed warrior turned toward Nidhan Singh. My husband moved quickly, his body a swirl of lightning-fast leaps and twists. He stabbed the man in his unprotected side, just as the man pierced his sword through my husband's heart. Nidhan Singh fell, and his murderer lurched before he, too, crashed to his death.

I jumped over countless bodies, unable to take my eyes off the sword extending from my husband's chest. The armor around my heart shattered to pieces. In that moment, I was certain my soul journeyed with my beloved husband's spirit as it left his body. *No one is ours. We all belong to Waheguru.*

Grief-stricken, I lost focus—a fatal error. A searing pain shot through my left side. A soldier had seized the opportunity to stab me in the stomach, and I collapsed to the ground next to my husband. I pressed my left hand against the wound and felt the warmth of my blood as it oozed out. My attacker, confident in his kill, walked away. I did not see the face of the man who struck me, and it didn't matter. What mattered was Nidhan Singh, his body still warm in my arms, unresponsive to my touch. I tried to withdraw the sword from his chest but I was in too much pain.

"Teri meri ikk jindri, Nidhan Singh. In this lifetime and every one after, you will always be my one love," I whispered as I felt myself fading.

Some of Wazir Khan's soldiers clamored as they surrounded the well. Frustrated to find there was no water, they yelled at each other before storming off in a fit of anger. My plan had worked, but at what cost? From what I could see, no Khalsa men were left standing. I knew Dilbagh had fallen as well. *My loyal, steadfast veer. Gone.*

*Is the Guru safe?*

I needed help but couldn't muster up the strength to speak. And even if I could call out, no one would hear me. I'd be gone before they found me.

I shivered as I lay in the dirt. A deep chill settled over the battleground, making it hard to breathe. The wind cut through me like an icy dagger. *Enter death in peace. You're almost free.* I closed my eyes to shield against the sun's glare and awaited death's arrival.

*Waheguru, help me.* And then, like a falling raindrop becoming one with the vast ocean, my mind diffused into something much larger than myself. It pulled me away from the battlefield. Peace illuminated my soul, offering me release from my earthly shackles.

For the first time, it became clear to me what our oppressors felt. They felt fear: the fear of defeat, which would make them insignificant. They felt fear of the unknown because it might threaten them or their loved ones. And this is a feeling much of humankind knows. I, too, had been held captive by the fear of facing my destiny. And now, I embraced my purpose, though it came at a great price. My dharam was to defend the Khalsa, the pure. Shivering, I held Nidhan Singh's hand as I slipped away from this world. I felt light as air as darkness descended.

Divinity engulfed me. Freedom was mine.

# SIXTEEN

As death cradled me, I heard a soothing voice repeating a blessing many times over. "Here lies my Khalsa. He commands twenty thousand. He commands thirty thousand. He rules the hearts of a hundred thousand. He takes many steps toward me, and he is blessed with happiness."

Then, I heard the voice ask, "Are you alive, my dear puttar? Can you hear me? It is I, your Guru. You saved many lives today, including mine." It was Guru Gobind Singh Ji's voice. *He is safe and unharmed!*

"Guru Ji, I am Mahan Singh," a warrior spoke up, struggling to find air. "I left your side at Anandpur Sahib, dear Guru, but I returned. We feared death, but now, I am at peace. Before I go, I beg you to tear up the letter we signed renouncing our loyalty to you. Please forgive us, Guru Ji."

The sound of papers rustled, as though they were being retrieved from a bag. Then I heard them being torn. The Guru must have thrown the ripped-up pieces to the wind, because a shred of paper flew above my head before blowing away.

"The letter has been destroyed. You are true Sikhs. I bless the men lost to us on the battlefield today as the Chali Mukte, forty liberated souls. This town shall now be named Muktsar, pool of liberation, in your honor." *My husband's honor has been redeemed, and his soul liberated.*

I thrust my ice-cold body upward with what little strength I could muster and attempted to reach the Guru. He looked in my direction in astonishment and hurried to my side. He squatted next to me, and the warmth of his presence melted away the frigidity and pain in my body.

He gently stroked my head. "Oh, my dhi! You have shown so much courage today. Let me take care of you until you recover. Then, I will help you return to your family."

"Guru Ji," I whispered, "I lost my husband and my veer today—my world has been shattered. I wish to stay with you instead."

"You are my daughter, and you will remain by my side."

Turning to his men, he shouted, "Veere, one of our warriors has survived, but she is injured. Come at once to help me take care of her!"

Two warriors rushed over and carried me to the camp uphill. They laid me down on a jute mat inside a tent.

The left side of my hip throbbed in pain, and I reached down to stanch the flow of blood.

"Don't touch it." One of the men gently moved my hand away. He then dabbed a wet cloth around the raw gash. I clasped my hands in pain. *Be strong, Bhag Kaur.* The man applied an herbal poultice. As he dressed my wound, the stinging pain of the medicine alternated with the soothing pressure of the cloth against my skin, playing a game of rotating bittersweet sensations.

Shortly after, two Sikhs entered the tent holding a wooden club, a stone mortar, and a box of assorted herbs. They ground cannabis leaves, poppy seeds, black pepper, almonds, and green cardamom into a paste, reciting a soft prayer as they worked. They scooped a portion of the paste into a clay vessel filled with water and mixed it.

One of them handed me the drink. "Drink this shaheedi degh. It will alleviate your pain."

I sat up and leaned to my right so as not to put any pressure on my left side. I lifted the vessel to my mouth, allowing the thick drink to slide down my throat, and then lay back. Soon, I entered a trance and fell into a deep, restful sleep.

"Nidhan Singh. Dilbagh Singh. Mahan Singh. Prahlad Singh . . ."

At sunrise, the remaining Khalsa warriors cremated their fallen comrades, reciting their names to honor their supreme sacrifice. I writhed in pain as the flames consumed the bodies of my beloved husband and brother, but my eyes were dry. A part of me had died with them on the battlefield, and now numbness pulsed within me.

After the ceremony, Chaupa Singh spoke to me, "You saved our Guru's life. Without the forty men you led into battle, the Khalsa army might not have survived this attack. It may be difficult for you to see this as a victory right now, but you won this battle for Sikhs everywhere." I smiled with the little strength I had.

A messenger was dispatched to inform family members of their loss. My heart shattered at the thought of my family and Nidhan Singh's mother receiving the worst news possible. I imagined my mother-in-law would live with her daughter in Amritsar and spend the rest of her days in peace. Mataji and Pitaji would help Harleen raise their grandson . . . and life would go on.

Guru Ji and his warriors continued to care for me in the days that followed. My physical body healed, but what of my heart, my soul? I yearned for my husband—the warmth of his body next to mine, his easy affection, the teasing glances we exchanged, and his wholehearted acceptance of who I was.

At night, the once peaceful dreams of my youth were snatched from my mind and replaced with blood and war. One nighttime affliction took me back to the battle in Muktsar. *The cold desert air circles my head like a vulture. My hands burn as I hold a flaming-hot kirpan. Enemy soldiers fly out of dark clouds; their mouths stretched in wicked grimaces. Hundreds attack me at once, and one stabs me in the heart. Nidhan Singh rushes over to me. I tell him with my final breath, "I could never lose you, so it is I who must go. I must save your life."*

Every night, I'd wake up drenched in sweat, my hair stuck to my temples, and my heart pounding deep in my chest. My breath came in bursts, short and fast. In the end, I'd curl up into a ball and cry myself back into a disturbed sleep. This nightly torture was worse than any opponent I faced in battle.

One morning, having gained enough strength to walk, I stepped outside my camp tent, still tired from nighttime's torment. I didn't talk to anyone about my nightmares. Everyone there had engaged in battle. I doubted they had many nights of peaceful rest either.

Chaupa Singh was shucking corn. He scooped up handfuls of sand into a pot over a chulha and buried the cobs in the sand, rotating the pieces now and then to evenly roast them.

Behind him, the rising sun hung low on the horizon. But the sight failed to captivate me when being alive was this painful. Jeeti would have said I was being bitter, like karela. I missed her.

The sound of footsteps brought me back to the present. The Guru approached me as though he knew I needed him. My body relaxed instantly, bathed in his love. I bowed my head in respect. He was carrying two sugarcane stalks, and he handed me one. We chewed in silence, savoring the sweet respite it provided.

"Dhi, your devotion to me is pure. May you remain blessed." He placed his hand on my head.

Tears streamed down my face. "You were there for me in my time of need, as the protector of the meek. And you love me as your dhi, Divine One."

A small smile brightened his face. "Do you not see that you, too, are divine?" His hand remained on my head. "The divinity that is within me lies within you as well. When my men deserted me, you brought them back. You lost everyone you loved fighting for your faith. Your loyalty and purity of heart are beyond measure. It would honor me if you would remain by my side as a bodyguard."

My joy bubbled over like a pot of milk on the boil. In his most painful time, the Guru gave me hope and purpose. I felt his divine love light up within me.

*Bhag Bhari, how fortunate have you been this whole time?*

We left Muktsar and traveled southeast to the town of Talwandi Sabo, where we set up a temporary camp. There, I was formally inducted as a member of the Guru's innermost circle. The Khalsa began to lovingly refer to me as Mai Bhago. Mata Bhag Kaur. I was now a mother of many.

I permanently adopted the blue and orange garb of a Khalsa warrior. Every morning, I would wrap my saffron-colored dastaar with utmost devotion. I armed myself with a large lance and heavy musket.

In Talwandi Sabo, the Guru poured himself into consolidating the Guru Granth Sahib Ji, a compendium of our holiest scripture. Most days, he labored from morning until night, deep in study. Scholars, artists, and poets came from all over to assist him in his endeavor. Listening to their eternal words rid me of any remaining fear, and I finally stopped having nightmares.

The fiery letter our Guru had written to Aurangzeb touched the emperor's heart, so he invited the Guru to Delhi. The Guru set out to meet him, accompanied by his most loyal Sikhs. But soon after we left, we received news that the emperor had died of old age. In the succession of wars that followed, the Khalsa helped one of his sons, Bahadur Shah, secure the throne. The new emperor met Guru Gobind Singh Ji, and they traveled south together. We pitched camp at Nanded on the Godavari River, but the emperor did not stay, continuing his travels.

Our new camp was surrounded by lush greenery. The alluvial river soil was rich and moist, ideal for growing crops. I could not wait to plant sugarcane. We were blissfully unaware of trouble brewing far from Nanded.

One day, the Guru was resting in his tent after prayer, when a guttural scream shook the camp. The sound of metal upon metal clanged like thunder. Someone was trying to kill the Guru! His bodyguards rushed into the tent, bodies pressing against each other as we pushed through the crowd. My nostrils filled with the smell of blood, and my stomach turned. Then, mayhem reigned.

"Chaa!"

The Guru lifted his sword and brought it down on his bull-faced attacker, steel cleaving flesh. The force of the blow nearly took the man's head off, and he fell, dead before he hit the ground.

Blood gushed from a gaping wound just below the Guru's heart. He clutched his chest as everyone in the tent froze in shock. Even in mortal danger, he looked peaceful, a divine light outlining his presence. His gaze rested on me, giving me the strength I needed to act.

"There is another intruder!" I snapped to attention. A man cloaked in green attempted to sneak out of the tent. His head was lowered and his pace frantic.

I charged through the chaotic jumble. "Coward!" I shouted, causing everyone to turn in my direction.

The attacker unsheathed his sword, which I knocked from his hands, just as another warrior drove his blade through the man's heart. Blood sprayed from his wound, and he fell backward, slamming his head on the ground. *How could we allow the Guru to be in harm's way?*

I scrambled back to reach the Guru. "Veere, move away. Do not crowd him."

We cleaned and dressed his wound, but the cuts were so deep that we struggled to stanch the bleeding. *Apply pressure. Apply pressure. Apply pressure.* We prayed that he would make it until surgeons could mend him.

Hearing the news, Emperor Bahadur Shah sent his personal surgeons to administer to the Guru, and he recovered. His wound seemed to heal well. After that day, I never left the Guru's side.

Not long after his attack, a sudden peace washed over me while on guard outside his tent. I thought of how the Guru made me feel like family. His love for me was unlike any other. It didn't carry expectation or judgment but acceptance. If my love for Nidhan Singh was the warmth of the sun, and my love for my parents and veere a place of comfort, then what I felt for the Guru was a cooling dip in a moonlit stream. I had been blessed by the gift of his love.

*I am the Guru's bodyguard. How do you describe a feeling that cannot be expressed by mere language? Imagine one whom you would die for. Imagine someone attempts to harm them. You stand in the way to take the deadly blow upon yourself. Focus on that moment you step forward and feel the full force of that love in your soul, protective and resolute. He is pure love.*

We learned that General Wazir Khan, jealous of the emperor's conciliatory treatment of the Guru, had sent two spies to assassinate the Guru. They entered the camp at Nanded under the guise of bringing gifts of horses. Such visitors were common, and these two had seemed completely innocuous.

Aware of the chaos encircling this deadly encounter and the continued risk of attack, Guru Gobind Singh Ji passed the leadership of Sikhs to the newly compiled Holy Book, the Guru Granth Sahib Ji, ending the line of mortal leaders.

Soon after, his strength restored, Guru Gobind Singh Ji lifted a bow. We watched with apprehension as he nocked an arrow and pulled the string. The strain stretched his wound, and he began to bleed. The bleeding would not subside, and we knew he didn't have long in this world.

And then, my beloved Guru merged with the Light.

Why did I lose everyone I loved? My thoughts began to spiral, when something lifted me up. How lucky were those who dwelled within Him! I felt free, joyous even, and at complete peace.

Love encircled me.

# EPILOGUE

The period after the tenth Guru's passing was marked by a long and bitter war between the Sikhs and the Mughal empire. A valiant warrior named Banda Singh Bahadur avenged the attack on the Guru by defeating the general behind the cowardly assassination attempt and established a Sikh nation, returning the land to its people. This act put him on a collision course with Emperor Bahadur Shah, and they continued to battle for control in Punjab and beyond.

My role in the Khalsa army began and ended with Guru Gobind Singh Ji. Content that I had fulfilled my dharam, I settled into a restful life. I traveled south to Janwara, where they needed teachers. I taught until my hair turned the color of a steel blade and my feet cautioned me to tread lightly. But it didn't matter that time had passed. I could still taste the dirt of the battlefield, feel the clutch of fear, hear the screams of men, and smell death and the smoke of ashes.

Worship gave me peace.

One morning, while deep in meditation under the shade of a banyan tree, a strange feeling came over me. Through the darkness, I entered a world full of color. A streak of orange and blue brought me to Muktsar, and old feelings of loss returned. The sky darkened, and in front of me, a wondrous gurdwara appeared, its dome illuminated in starlight. A vast lake, a sarovar, stretched out in the desert, so large that it could easily hold a village within it. Thousands of Sikhs had gathered to celebrate their faith. They took dips in the sacred lake and feasted on rauh di kheer, sweet rice cooked in sugarcane juice. A man's voice rang out, louder than a musket, "Chali Mukte! Waheguru Ji Ka Khalsa! Waheguru Ji Ki Fateh!" *Could it be that the forty men who sacrificed their lives that day are remembered as martyrs by future generations?*

I plunged into darkness again.

When the light returned, I stood in front of a painting of a female Sikh warrior. I squinted, trying to focus on the face. And then I froze. The woman in the artwork was me. I was commanding my troops at Muktsar, dressed in the Khalsa Swarupa. One hand held a mighty kirpan, and the other grasped an iron shield and spear. I sat atop a horse on raised ground. In front of me, forty men were arrayed in battle formation. *Would I be revered as a great warrior?*

I felt light like a feather in the wind. And to my enormous joy, the future began to whisper stories of other brave Sikh women.

A woman who was a military mastermind assumed leadership of the Kanhaiya Misl. She transformed into a warrior and commanded an army of thousands of horsemen, laying the foundation for a Sikh empire. She was the force behind the rise of a great Sikh emperor of Hindustan, Maharaja Ranjit Singh.

She addressed me directly, "I am Sada Kaur, Mai Bhago. You were my light and my guide. Your bravery propelled mine!" With these words, she disappeared into a swirl of color.

A young Sikh princess appeared before me, seated beside an older man, presumably her grandfather. The man resembled Baba Ala Singh, a great ruler of Patiala. This princess grew up to rule over a kingdom comprising hundreds of villages. I watched as she received news from a messenger—a cousin, a king of a neighboring region, was in trouble. This lionhearted princess led three thousand warriors to rescue her veer. Later in life, she defended the city of Patiala against powerful forces. This leader possessed all the virtues of a warrior—courage, perseverance, and sagacity.

"Mai Bhago, I am Bibi Rajinder Kaur. I am humbled to be in the presence of the legendary savior of Sikhism." She bowed in respect and vanished.

Another flash, and I was transported to a new location. A squat, white building sat on an expanse of land larger than the fields of my childhood village. In front was a bronze statue of a female warrior seated on a horse, wielding a kirpan.

Inscribed on the facade was a line of scripture: *May I never refrain from righteous acts.* Below this were the words, "Mai Bhago Armed Forces Preparatory Institution for Girls." *A school is named after me?*

I turned to see a formation of female cadets marching in a straight line toward me. They were dressed in earth-colored uniforms with red sashes. The soldiers wore crimson hats, not turbans, on their heads. I floated inside the building, where young women were being taught to use firearms. These women wanted to be trained as warriors, as I did when I was a kuri, and a school in my name allowed them to pursue their dreams.

I felt an inexplicable connection to these women. Perhaps we were cast from the same mold. A mold that created women ready to bear arms to defend their beliefs and loved ones, willing to lay down their lives for justice.

Then, darkness surrounded me for the last time. I floated upward, my mind in a state of absolute equanimity. I looked down at my fingers, and they appeared to be translucent. Above, a light shimmered, resplendent in its beauty, its warmth filling me with joy. My memories faded like salt slipping through my fingers. I saw my pitaji and mataji beaming at me, Chotu and Dilbagh playfully wrestling each other, and my mamaji and mamiji holding hands, with Gurdas and Jasmeet by their side. Jeeti smiled broadly in my direction. Nidhan Singh's kind eyes locked onto mine. Their love wrapped its warmth around me. I became love. And then, we were one.

# A NOTE FROM THE AUTHOR

I began writing this book in 2017, a few years before we'd faced the coronavirus pandemic. In the five years since then, my labor of love has evolved into the book it is today. The purpose was always to reach you—my readers.

As a child, I grew up listening to stories about our cherished Gurus at the gurdwara. Their deep spirituality, strong character, and bravery enamored me. But, in hearing these stories, and more recently when delving into historical texts, I was left unsatisfied by the few historical details of Sikh women. It wasn't as though Sikhism didn't have powerful, complex women. So, I decided to give voice to a woman I'd always admired: Mai Bhago.

Mai Bhago is a revered warrior saint in Sikhism, the fifth-largest religion in the world. Sikhs believe in one God, equality, freedom of religion, and community service. In the early 1700s, Mai Bhago and her battalion of forty men, the Chali Mukte, fought the Mughal army at Khidrana. This was the tenth Guru's final battle—the Battle of Muktsar. These larger-than-life heroes with inspiring virtues etched morals into many other Sikhs, including me. Mai Bhago's valor is said to have saved the Guru's life, which allowed him to compile the Holy Book, the Guru Granth Sahib Ji. This compendium is the most sacred Sikh text and serves as the final and eternal Guru for Sikhs. Mai Bhago helped Guru Gobind Singh Ji lay the foundation for Sikhism. That is monumental to me.

I also wanted to understand her as a woman. As a young adult, I craved a story about someone with a shared background with me. I thought, if I ever wrote a book, a Sikh woman would be at the forefront of the action. And if I told it in her voice, showing her triumphs and heartbreak, we'd see the unique way she viewed her place in the world.

We included the word "Lioness" in the book's title because Kaur, the title taken by Sikh women, means princess or lioness. Their male counterparts are called Singhs, lions. Both of these titles signify strength and courage. Sikhs have a long martial history in India, from the days of the Gurus through colonization, and as soldiers in the Indian military today.

There were many more Sikh female warriors in history, including, but certainly not limited to, Sada Kaur, Bibi Rajinder Kaur, Maharani Jind Kaur, Bibi Sahib Kaur, and Mai Sukhan. Today, Sikh women are considered equal to the men in the community in every way. Mutual respect thrives between the genders. I believe this was largely due to the strides made by women like Mai Bhago centuries ago.

My love for Sikhi stems from my mother. She taught herself the Gurmukhi script and read the Holy Book in its entirety. She narrated stories to my sisters and me and taught us shabads and prayer songs. She even drafted her own book, a compilation of some of her favorite prayer hymns and stories. I like to think of it as her spiritual journal. In her book, she had written shabads in Gurmukhi and then translated them into English for her daughters. For every male pronoun in the original, my mother substituted "s/he" in English. When I think of Mai Bhago, I think of my mother—a strong, faithful, and loving woman, transcendent of the ages.

As we know, there is learning in history. In sharing Mai Bhago's story, I believe she will inspire courage in a time when I've seen many frightened about social injustice. We find hope in the challenges faced by others and realize we can rise through our difficult times. And ultimately, it is our humanity and bravery that will save us.

In writing this story, I tried to present history as truthfully as possible. I filled in the blanks in a way that seemed fitting to a woman of Mai Bhago's greatness. The day-to-day events in her life were fictional; however, events such as the gathering of Sikhs at Anandpur Sahib and the Battle at Muktsar are based on historical facts. Some of the main characters have been drawn from my imagination, including Jeeti, Gurdas, Bhag Kaur's mamaji and mamiji, her mother-in-law, Harleen, Chaupa Singh, and more. I was unable to find historical references to Mai Bhago's children, but she is said to have married a Nidhan Singh from the village of Patti. I apologize in advance to historians and scholars of Sikhism.

The following references were invaluable in writing this book:

Chaudhuri, B. B.,*Peasant History of Late Pre-Colonial and Colonial India*. India: Pearson Education, 2008.

Macauliffe, Max Arthur. *The Sikh Religion: Its Gurus, Sacred Writings, and Authors, Vol 5*. United Kingdom: Cambridge University Press, 2014.

Singh, Daljeet, and Singh, Kharak, eds.,*Sikhism, Its Philosophy and History*. India: Institute of Sikh Studies, 1997.

Singh, Guru Gobind. *Zafarnama*. Translated by Navtej Sarna. India: Penguin India, 2011.

Singh, Harjit. *The Warrior Princess 2: The Moving Story of Guru Gobind Singh through the Eyes of Four Saintly Sikh Warrior Women*. India: Sikh-Heroes.com, 2003.

Singh, Khushwant. *A History of the Sikhs, Volume 1: 1469–1838*. India: Oxford University Press, 2nd edition, 2005.

Singh, Patwant. *The Sikhs*. New York: Image, 2001.

Singh, Surinder Jit. *The Masters and the World Divine*. Amristar, India: B. Chattar Singh Jiwan Singh, 1999.

Stronge, Susan, ed.,*The Arts of the Sikh Kingdoms*. United Kingdom: V&A Publications, 1999.

*https://www.thesikhencyclopedia.com*

# ACKNOWLEDGMENTS

Yuvraj and Shaan for being all mine. You are loved exactly as you are and for whom you will become.

Viney Kharbanda, my tough-love critic and practical voice, who doesn't always understand the creative process but humors me in mine.

Mom and Dad for believing in me endlessly and indulging my book-reading addiction. You taught me to respect books for the knowledge they impart, and I still place books on my head if one accidentally touches my foot. Mom's spiritual journal is, to date, the best work I have read and the greatest inspiration for my debut. Your unconditional love continues to guide me. Immensely.

Ritu and Renu for your positivity and easy sibling affection. I will always be "the goog" and "googster" to you both. I love that the source of the nickname was Nanima tenderly pinching my cheeks and calling me "googlie" in the back seat of mamaji's Ambassador in New Delhi. Love my nephews and nieces Celine, Dylan, Ayanna, Owen, and Arian, and my brothers-in-law.

My sister-in-law Neelam, my mother-in-law, father-in-law, and nephew Avi—love you deeply. You share savory Punjabi meals seasoned with the most important ingredient: love. We feel the prayers and blessings you send us.

Jennifer Lyons, my literary agent, and her team for their unwavering advocacy of my work. You parted the waters for me.

Ambika Sambasivan, the fiercest editor, for lifting this story up to the world.

Anantjeet Kaur, the brilliant cover artist, for depicting Mai Bhago in all her glory.

Preeti and Kalisha for being the kind of reader writers dream about.

Inni Kaur of the Sikh Research Institute for your generosity in verifying this story's historical accuracy.

Three cups of chai a day for giving me the energy to write all the words.

Thank you.